Her Dirty Secret

A Novella By Melanie A. Smith

Wicked Dreams Publishing

Published by
Wicked Dreams Publishing
Denton County, TX USA
info@wickeddreamspublishing.com

Paperback ISBN: 978-1-7330748-3-4

Table of Contents

Chapter 1 — Emily

"Do you ever want to get married?"

Chad looks up at me from the acoustic he's restringing. "You're the last person I ever expected to ask that question," he replies with a knowing smirk before going back to what he was doing.

"Hey, I might get married someday," I protest with a whine. "And you didn't answer the question." I lean forward on the glass counter, letting my feet swing freely as I await his reply. Not that I really care. But the shop is slow today, for a Saturday anyway, and the engagement party I'll be attending later is on my mind.

"I don't know. Maybe. I can't say I've given it much thought," he finally replies as he clips the newly wound strings and grabs a tuning fork.

I look him up and down. I've known Chad too long to think of him that way, but he's not bad looking. Mid-thirties, average height, average build, with sandy brown hair and light brown eyes. But he's one of the best guitarists I know, and chicks dig that. Well, chicks who haven't been there, done that, learned their lesson, got the T-shirt, and all that.

"Yeah, me neither," I agree.

He laughs. "Bullshit. All chicks think about it."

I frown, drop my feet back to the ground, and slug him on the arm as he tunes. "Don't be such a misogynist."

"What's this about, Emily?" he asks bluntly.

I'd cringe, but it's exactly what I like about having mostly guy friends. They don't beat around the bush.

"I'm going to my brother's engagement party today," I admit with a sigh. "I dunno. I'm happy for him. But it makes me realize I can't really see myself ever getting married. Is that weird?"

Chad shrugs as he finishes and puts the guitar back in the case. "Maybe you just haven't met the right person. Maybe go through another few hundred and you'll find 'The One,'" he replies with a cheeky grin.

"Fuck you, Chad."

"Heh heh," he chuckles. "Isn't that your flavor of the month's job?"

I glare daggers at him, but luckily he's saved from my wrath by a customer approaching the counter. He smiles serenely as I lead them to the pedals they're looking for, and I stick my tongue out at him as soon as their back is turned.

Probably better I didn't get to reply. Then I'd have to admit things with Jack went kaput last week. Like they always do, though this one lasted longer than most. Even though I wasn't all that interested in him. Not that I'm ever all that interested in any of them.

Most of the guys I meet are just guys. Little more than boys, and certainly not men. That's what I get for working in a music store. Hanging out with musicians. Being a musician. Hell, who am I kidding — I'm just as flighty and immature as most of the guys I date. But at least I don't pretend to be something else.

I shake myself, unsure of why I feel like such a Debbie Downer. I'm not usually this sad after a breakup. I push the thoughts out of my head and try to focus on the last hour of my shift. Before I have to put on a happy face for Bryce and Sera's party.

* * *

I get back to my apartment with little time until I have to get to the party, but I still take care primping. Even though I feel like crap, I decide I might as well look like a million bucks. I carefully wash and straighten my long, chestnut brown hair before applying the layers of makeup that will make the blue in my eyes really pop. Likewise, I pick a slinky, fitted dress that hugs my thin frame with splashes of bright spring colors, even though the cooling Seattle September air hints at the rapidly approaching fall.

Once I'm satisfied, I call for a car service and pick up my ukulele to practice while I wait. I'm not nearly as good on it yet as I am with a mandolin, but I'm getting there. It's hard to work in a music shop and not get distracted by all the cool instruments. My apartment is certainly a testament to that, with nearly a dozen littered around the living room. Not that I've ever spent much time getting particularly good at any of them. Much like in life, I flit among my instruments, playing whatever makes me happy at the moment.

My cellphone pings, interrupting my reverie, or practice, or whatever the hell you call it, and I head out to meet my car.

The drive through downtown and over the West Seattle bridge is uneventful. I glance out over the industrial district and watch a ferry chugging along slowly through the waters beyond. Not for the first time, I realize what a beautiful place I live in. But it hasn't stopped me from wanting to travel the world, if only for a little while.

I almost did, before my dad died unexpectedly. But then Mom needed me. And then Bryce had his accident, and he needed me. And now that he's healed, and he and Sera are getting engaged, I suspect there will be little nieces and nephews who need me soon.

As we start winding through the streets of my childhood, I put on my game face. *Time to act happy, Em, even if your own dreams are on hold. Whatever those might be.* I can't help laughing at myself a little. For a twenty-eight-year-old, you'd think I'd have my shit together better.

Once I'm out, the car peels off behind me and I trek up the front steps, taking a deep breath before entering. I head through the massive house to the kitchen, knowing it's where everyone probably is as they prepare for the onslaught of guests due to arrive shortly.

But I actually find Mom and Aunt Char in the living room, laying a tablecloth over a banquet table that's been lined against the wall. Bags of supplies sit behind them on the couches.

"Where are Bryce and Sera?" I pipe up.

Mom, who is facing me, looks up, but Aunt Char jumps a little in surprise. She turns around with a hand to her chest.

"Goodness, Emily, you startled me," she replies.

"They're in the kitchen, dear," my mother supplies.

I set my purse down on a side table and move toward my mother.

"Shouldn't they be doing all this?" I ask, planting a kiss on her cheek.

Aunt Char waves a hand. "Nonsense," she chides me. "We're here. Why wouldn't we help?"

With a shrug, I turn to head into the kitchen to give Bryce a hard time for resigning them to manual labor. Honestly.

As I swing the door open, I catch Bryce's huge frame wrapped around Sera in a corner of the kitchen.

"And this time, Em isn't going to spoil it," Bryce is telling her. He goes to kiss her, and I just can't help myself.

"Em isn't going to spoil what?" I ask unnecessarily loudly with the most innocent expression I can muster.

Sera looks up at me and bursts out laughing, letting her long, wavy light brown hair fall into her face. My brother's head whips around and he glares at me.

"Shitty timing, as usual, sis." And with that, he proceeds to ignore me, planting a far too steamy kiss on Sera. They go at it like teenagers, clearly not caring that I'm standing right here.

"You know, this is your party," I remind them. "You might want to help out a little. People will be here soon."

It takes a second, but they finally peel apart.

"If you insist," he replies, planting his giant, muscled self in front of me. I don't know why he thinks he can intimidate me like he does everyone else. I know exactly where to punch him to make him drop to the floor and cry like a girl.

With a smug smile, I pick up a stack of plates and cups. He does the same, following me back out to the living room.

As we lay everything out, I can't help poking at him a little. "Seriously, you gotta be more careful with the PDA," I tell him. "Would you want Mom to walk in on you guys feeling each other up like that?"

Bryce smirks down at me. "Jealous much?"

If I was teasing before, I'm annoyed now. "Uh, no."

He crosses his arms over his slab of a chest and raises an eyebrow at me. "Emily Hoyt, I think you *are* jealous," he teases me.

Something about my big brother and that tone of voice makes me want to stomp my foot. But I resist. Barely.

"Don't worry, little sis," he assures me, wrapping his huge arm around my neck. I give him a look that forbids the coming noogie, and thankfully he relents. "Someday, you'll find someone who is just as crazy about you as I am about her." He looks back at the kitchen wistfully.

It melts the fight out of me. "You two *are* ridiculously, adorably perfect for each other," I grudgingly admit. "But that doesn't mean I'm not just fine on my own."

"Of course you are," Aunt Char offers, coming back through the room with Mom behind her. "Emily has always been a free spirit. She doesn't need a man tying her down."

Mom shakes her head. "Says my never-married sister."

Bryce and I chuckle as they head into the kitchen.

"At least someone in this family gets me," I shoot at him.

Bryce narrows his eyes at me. "Oh, believe me, I get that you don't want to be tied down to anything traditional. The dozen times you've turned down working in the family business to pursue your 'music career' pretty much got that point across." He says it with a smile. And I realize I'm just being a grouch. Because if anyone gets me, loves me, accepts me for who I am, it's my steadfast big brother. He's always been the reliable rock of the family, even more so than Dad was. Dad was just as moody as I am. At least I know it's genetic. Not that that helps much.

But before I can apologize for being so snippy, there's a knock on the door. Bryce goes to answer, but I wave at him to continue setting up, and I head down the hall and into the foyer.

I open the door to a completely average-looking middle-aged man and a tiny redhead. The man extends his hand.

"Kent Evans," he introduces himself. "I'm Sera's dad. And this is my wife, Barb."

I shake his hand, wincing under his vice grip. "I'm Emily, Bryce's sister," I reply, offering my hand to Barb next. Her handshake is just as firm and uncomfortable. Yeesh. These two. I step back in invitation. "Please, come in." They enter, standing awkwardly in the foyer. Since I'm not sure we're ready for them in the living room, I decide to leave them here. "I'll just go get Sera."

I make a break for it down the hall and through the living room, where Bryce gives me a weird look as I dash by him into the kitchen.

"Hey, Sera, your dad and his wife are here," I hiss.

She looks up from talking to Mom and Aunt Char, clearly startled. "Already?"

Sera whips past me, heading out the kitchen door. Mom and Aunt Char look at me, and I shrug. Not a moment later, Bryce pops in.

"Aunt Charlotte, can you please man the front door? We're trying to keep Sera's brother and father apart until he's ready to, er, tell his dad something."

"Of course," she agrees, following him out.

Mom and I exchange a look.

"I think it's best if I go play hostess as well," Mom says wisely. "Why don't you start putting out the food, Emily?"

"Sure thing," I agree.

I start moving dishes from the loaded counters to the banquet table, which unfortunately doesn't allow me to catch much of the conversation with Sera's dad and his wife. I have to admit that I'm more than curious, since Sera's told me all about the double life her dad apparently lived with this woman while she was a kid, but I figure it's better not to be caught eavesdropping. And not to annoy Mom by neglecting to feed people. Heaven forbid.

Once everything is out, I note that the place is pretty packed. Looks like most people are here. I make the rounds, introducing myself to everyone, making sure they know where to find the food, and all that kind of stuff. Being fake and cheery isn't really my thing, and my dangerously low brain-to-mouth filter means that I need to avoid talking to anyone in particular for too long.

And when a couple with a baby arrive, I introduce myself briefly and then make sure I stay as far away as possible. It's something I would never admit to anyone, but babies freak me out.

I babysat a baby once when I was a teenager. That's all it took. The little hellion spent the whole time throwing up, peeing, pooping, or screaming. Sometimes more than one of those at a time. And when he peed *in my mouth* I swore from then on never again. No babies. No pretending to like people's babies. Probably not even having my own babies, a conviction that developed steam over the years. And even though this baby looks happy and cute in a little sailor outfit, I just can't. Traumatized for life.

So when I hear the doorbell chime, knowing Aunt Char is in the middle of a conversation, I more than happily trot down the hall and away from anything baby to answer it.

What I was in no way expecting is the Roman god standing on the doorstep. Lean and sculpted in perfectly tailored black pants and a black button-front shirt, with a perfectly styled head of gorgeous dark hair and a trimmed beard, brown eyes sparkling like he knows exactly how outrageously dazzling he is, I know without a doubt who this must be. The lying, cheating Italian prick who fucked with Sera's heart. Who my brother hates with every fiber of his being. Well, as much as Bryce Hoyt can hate anyone. When my mild-mannered, all-knowing big brother hates someone, that's saying something. But fuck me sideways if this isn't the most gorgeous man I've ever laid eyes on.

He stares at me expectantly as I stand there, speechless, looking me up and down in a way that makes it even harder to form a sentence.

I'm saved having to string words together in greeting when Sera appears behind me.

"Alessandro," she breathes, a little too happily.

"*Buona sera*," he offers in return, extending his hands as he steps across the threshold. My heart hammers in my chest at the voice that's just as sexy as he is. They greet each other with a hug, just as my brother walks in behind Sera, clearly struggling to hide his distaste at her obviously being glad to see him.

But as much as I hate the dude for what he did to her, I kind of get it. They've been through a lot together. And Sera's a smart chick, even if she does tend to overlook people's shortcomings. But damn, I might be willing to overlook his shortcomings too if he's half as good in bed as he is gorgeous. The odds are good as, from what I hear, he's had enough practice.

I blush furiously, banishing the thought as I watch them converse. I swear Alessandro's eyes wander to me more than is natural, but I could just be imagining it. Or I could just be staring so hard that I'm making him uncomfortable.

I realize suddenly it's been a long time since I've had good sex. I'm sure that's where this is coming from. Just horniness. I shake myself a little and make to head back into the living room when there's another knock on the door.

Since Bryce is closer, he answers, grabbing Sera's attention too, as it's her brother and his boyfriend. That leaves Alessandro on my side of the foyer. And apparently, I haven't stopped staring at him despite my intention to leave.

He turns to me and sizes me up once more.

"I'm sorry, I didn't catch your name," he says silkily. "Are you a friend of Serafina's?"

"How rude of me," I reply, finally finding my voice, and my manners. I extend a hand. "I'm Emily. And yes, I'm friends with Sera. Though I'm also Bryce's sister."

Alessandro accepts my hand, tilting his head and raising an eyebrow, a smirk playing at his mouth as he brings the back of my hand to his lips. His full, delicious lips. He places a light kiss there before raising his eyes back to mine.

"Are you, now?" he asks, still holding my hand in his. "Then perhaps I shouldn't find you quite so beautiful. I fear your brother already doesn't like me much."

I've been fed enough lines in my day to know an attempt to get in my pants when I hear one. Though I know that's probably exactly what he's doing, his words sound much more sincere than not. Or maybe I just find him that attractive. And it has been more than a year since he and Sera split. And she is engaged to my brother now. Would she really care if we had a fling? Though it's Alessandro's implication that's more to the point — my brother would care. And that, unfortunately, is an issue. I wander down the hall, and he follows.

"No, I'm afraid he doesn't," I agree. "And I wouldn't want to get you in trouble. I know Sera cares for you very much."

A feline smile spreads across his lips as we settle onto a vacant love seat in the living room. "Yes, we will always care for each other," he agrees. "And I'm glad to see her so happy. But still, I think I would happily face the giant to get to know you."

A peal of laughter escapes me. "You call him 'the giant'?" I ask, clapping in delight. "That's the best thing I've heard all day." It fits Bryce, to a T. He's such a towering, glowering fuddy-duddy sometimes. Especially when he gets in protective mode, which is not infrequently, and I'm sure something Alessandro saw a lot of.

Alessandro stares at me intently, looking like he wants to reach out for my face.

"What?" I ask self-consciously. "Do I have something on me?" I wipe at my mouth, suddenly worried there might be cheese dip lingering from the appetizers I snuck earlier.

"No," he replies lowly. "Forgive the cliché, but you're mesmerizing."

"Mhm," I reply, pressing my lips together in a skeptical glare. "I've heard about you. The whole handsome and charming shtick isn't going to work on me."

Now it's his turn to laugh unreservedly, and I can't decide which I like better, the stoic and sexy face, or the amused and joyful one. Mesmerizing. It's a good word, for him at least. I see why Sera was so hesitant about him in the beginning. He naturally just comes on strong. Luckily — or unluckily perhaps, for him — charisma doesn't really sway me. Because I'm not looking for a prince to sweep me off my feet into happily ever after. All I care about is having fun. Charisma isn't a requirement, though damned if he doesn't seem like fun too. If only it wouldn't give my brother the exact excuse he needed to do what I know he's been itching to do for the better part of two years and end the guy.

"Well, this is a first," he replies, still smiling.

"Oh? How's that?" I ask, honestly curious.

He leans in, his mouth hovering near my ear. "It seems you have the upper hand," he says softly. A shiver glides down my back. The accent, the heat emanating from him, his scent all prove him wrong. If he asked me to go upstairs right now, I'd be hard-pressed to refuse him. I fail to see how that gives me the upper hand.

"Mmmm," I hum, neither agreeing nor disagreeing.

The sound of tapping on a glass rips through whatever retort I was trying to form, and the room stills. Bryce stands on the other end, Sera at his side.

"Thank you, everyone, for coming," he says. "Sera and I are touched that you were all able to make it on such short notice. You all know that I proposed to this beautiful woman two weeks ago, and she accepted."

Cheers erupt, and a genuine smile crosses my face. I really am so happy for them. My brother holds up his hand to quiet the crowd.

"But you may not know I actually bought the ring a year ago." He shares a loving look with Sera that brings tears to my eyes. "And though fate prevented me from giving it to her until now, I've loved her since the day I met her. And I'm the luckiest bastard on the planet because she loves me too."

He pauses to kiss her, and something inside me rips. I suddenly feel like I need air. Unfortunately, he's not done.

"But if we've learned anything through it all, it's not to take for granted that there will be a tomorrow. So we promised each other that we would live each day with no regrets, without hesitation, without fear. Together. And because we didn't want to waste one more minute without joining our lives, we were married yesterday by a justice of the peace."

My gasp joins those around me. Including Alessandro's. As my brother continues, I can't help noticing Alessandro looks paler than he was. And I wonder if he's really over Sera, even after all this time. It helps me to not focus on my reaction to their news, which, if I'm being honest, isn't all good. It makes me uncomfortable in a way I don't want to think too hard about. It's nothing on them. They're perfect. But then, my brother has always been the perfect child. Me, not so much. And their perfect love for each other is a small, needling reminder of that.

"And so, I'd like to introduce you all to my wife — Serafina Hoyt." Bryce raises a glass, his eyes never leaving Sera. "Thank you, baby, for bringing me back and making me the happiest man alive. Never forget how much I love you." He slips a wedding ring out of his pocket, making a show of putting it on. And they kiss again.

God, my brother is married. This is so weird. I tear my eyes from them, looking back at Alessandro. He's still watching them with an inscrutable expression. I lay a hand on his arm.

"You okay?" I ask softly.

He turns to me, tears filling his eyes. "Yes," he manages. "I know it may seem strange to you, but they're tears of joy." I look at him, confused, and he laughs. "Really. I love her, truly, so how can they be anything but?" He squeezes my hand and slips away, joining the forming line to congratulate them. I watch for a moment in shock.

He sounds nothing like the selfish bastard I expected him to be. Big ol' flirt, absolutely. But there's something about his reaction that was so heartfelt and sincere. Knowing I won't be missed, that I can offer my congratulations later, I slip out the front door to absorb things alone. Sinking onto the steps, I stare up at the sky. Behind the bank of grey clouds, night has fallen. I breathe deeply of the cool air, letting it calm me.

It's hard to say what unnerved me more: that Bryce and Sera went off and did the deed, or Alessandro's selfless happiness for them. No, I know what is harder to come to terms with. To be fair, I only met the man myself tonight, but Sera confided in me at length over the end of their relationship. I was there to see what he did to her. Reconciling that with the man I saw crying for her happiness has shaken me.

I have to work to place my feelings. The closest I can get is that it gives me hope. That it's never too late to be someone else. Or maybe, even the person you always wanted to be. If Alessandro can change, grow, and move forward, then anything is possible.

It makes me realize that everyone around me is moving forward with their lives, while I've been stuck in the same place for years. In the same rut of partying, drinking, dating in the same crowd I've always run in. The wishers, the wanters, the dreamers. I'm all of those things. But I also want to be a doer. It makes me realize that it's time to start doing the things I've always hoped to do. To stop letting life derail me. Because if not now, when?

I rise and march back inside. And run smack into Alessandro.

"*Scusa,*" he gasps, grabbing me by the arms before I can topple over. I lean into the wall behind me to steady myself, and he lets go. But he doesn't move away. Staring up into his eyes, I decide he's one of the things I want to do. And I won't let my brother derail me. It's none of his business, and in any case, I never bring home any of the men I date anyway.

"Sorry," I say breathlessly. "I didn't mean to—"

"No, it was my fault I—"

I reach for him, silencing him with a hand on his arm. "It's okay." The heat of his gaze makes me blush, and I retract my hand, dropping it down and playing nervously with the ends of my hair. The humidity outside has curled them, and I tug at my hair, futilely trying to smooth it back into submission.

"Emily," he says. My name sounds beautiful on his lips. But then, I imagine everything does. I look up at him from under my eyelashes to see he's smoldering down at me. It's almost too much to take.

"Yes?" I prompt, swallowing hard.

"I just came to see if you were all right," he replies, stepping back slightly. "I saw you leave but couldn't break away. You seemed upset."

There he goes with the selflessness again. He's either a pile of contradictions, or he isn't the same man he once was. Part of me wants to forget about him, to not take the risk. But part of me wants to know him, and not just to know if people can really change.

I breathe deeply and right myself, dropping the coy flirtatious act. "Thank you," I reply. "But I'm fine. Or I will be."

Alessandro smiles indulgently at me. "You're a tempestuous one, aren't you?" he asks, a note of teasing in his voice.

I laugh shortly. "Yes, I suppose I am," I admit. "You also seem a little…" I try to come up with a word to describe him.

"Passionate," he murmurs. "That's the word you're looking for." I swallow hard again. It's not exactly where I was going, but clearly true, nonetheless.

We stare at each other for a moment.

"So you're really sure you'd be willing to deal with my brother just to get to know me?" I ask abruptly.

He gives me a mischievous smile. "Are you falling for the 'handsome and charming shtick' after all?"

I laugh. "Let's just say I've reconsidered. I realized I need to be more spontaneous and stop sitting around wishing things would happen a certain way."

"Intriguing," he replies, rubbing his finger under his chin with a sparkle in his eye.

A noise grabs my attention, and I look down the hall at the crowd starting to break up and head this way. With a sigh, I realize I'm out of time for now.

"I should go congratulate the happy couple," I tell him. "And then call my ride home. It was nice to meet you, Alessandro."

His eyes sweep over my face. "It was my pleasure, truly, Emily," he replies, stepping aside to let me pass. I walk away, thoroughly confused and disconcerted by our exchange. I can't even seem to flirt properly these days.

With a sigh, I seek Bryce and Sera out, giving them hugs and congratulations. They remind me that they'll be leaving for their honeymoon later tonight, and it makes me yearn for the kind of trip they're about to embark upon. And when I see them sneak away, it makes me yearn for what I know they're about to do.

It's a few more minutes until everyone clears out, and I spend the time cleaning up so Mom and Aunt Char don't have to. I say my goodnights and step outside to summon my ride and wait in the cool of the evening, rather than keep Mom and Aunt Char up.

But there's still a car in the driveway. And Alessandro sits on the hood of the sleek, dark luxury coupe.

"If I owned a car like that I wouldn't sit on the hood," I remark drily, pocketing my phone.

He grins widely. "What good is it if you can't?" he replies, hopping down.

I laugh, shaking my head. "What are you still doing here?"

He gestures to the car. "You said you needed a ride. Your chariot awaits."

His choice of words freezes me on the spot. "I'm not a damsel in distress," I snap.

Alessandro presses his lips together, clearly amused by my change of mood. It pushes me further into annoyed and I fold my arms over my chest.

"Do you get tired?" he asks with a tilt of his head.

"Of what?" I brace myself, expecting the pickup line that's probably coming.

But he steps forward, prying my arms away from my chest, holding my hands in his. "Of fighting against what you really want."

He might as well have poured a bucket of ice water over my head for how shocked his words leave me.

"You're right," I whisper, more to myself than him.

His hand slips under my chin, prompting me to look up into his eyes. "I know."

I give him a mock frown. "And you're arrogant."

He laughs. "I know that too."

His honesty makes me laugh with him. "I'll let you drive me home on one condition," I say with a sneaky smile.

"Go on," he replies.

"Show me what this baby can do."

With a grin, he walks around and opens the passenger door for me. I slide into the buttery-soft red leather seat. And when he gets in and takes off, holy shit does it take off. It takes half the time it usually would to get home, and I can barely direct him there for laughing gleefully as he whips around at high speeds.

As he idles outside of my building, the adrenaline speaks for me.

"Come upstairs," I say.

He looks over at me intently.

"Any other time I would," he says carefully, "but I must be on a flight to Napoli in a couple hours."

Shit. That's right. The whole reason Bryce and Sera are honeymooning in Italy is because she'd originally planned to go on a group trip to the Amalfi Coast with Alessandro.

"Ah, yes, that," I reply. "Some other time then." I give him a wan smile. "Thanks for the ride." I turn to leave, but he leans over and covers the hand I have on the door latch with his. I turn toward him, and his face is dangerously close to mine.

"Give me your phone," he says urgently.

I only hesitate for a moment before handing it over. He quickly programs something in, then hits a button. His phone, tucked behind the stick shift, vibrates. He presses another button, then hands it back.

"Now you have my number, and I have yours. I'll call you when I have a moment," he promises.

That one I've definitely heard before. "Yeah, okay," I reply, unconvinced. "Bye then."

He laughs and shakes his head. "You'll see." He gives me a wink but doesn't stop me leaving this time.

Chapter 2 — Emily

I'm not even in the apartment for five minutes when he calls.

"I'm an idiot," he says without preamble.

"I won't disagree with that," I reply. "A pretty girl asks you to have sex with her and you say no." I tsk at him.

He laughs loudly. "Well, I wasn't sure that's what you were asking, but I guess I am now."

I shake my head. "Is that why you called? To ask what I meant by, 'Come upstairs?'" I tease. "I know there might be something of a language barrier, but—"

"Come to Italy with me," he interrupts. And I'm rendered speechless. "I'm downstairs. You wanted to be spontaneous, no?"

My heartbeat thuds in my ears. I should have a million questions.

But I don't.

"Give me five minutes."

"Is that five minutes in real time or woman time?"

"You've already wasted thirty seconds asking me that," I reply in mock indignation. And I hang up.

I look around my apartment. Can I really do this? Can I really jet off to a foreign country at the last minute with a ridiculously hot Italian man I just met a few hours ago?

Even asking the questions in my head makes me laugh.

Hell. Yes.

I don't waste any more time thinking. I bolt into the bedroom, unearth my passport from the bottom of my desk drawer, thanking God I got one just in case, dig the suitcase out of my closet, and pack every loose article of clothing I can get my hands on, finishing with all of my toiletries and electronics. I also throw a few books into my purse for good measure. I race downstairs faster than I knew possible. And he's really there, leaning against the car.

When he sees me, he beams. "That was seven minutes, but I'll forgive you."

I throw him a mock glare. "You realize this is crazy, right?"

He crosses the distance between us quickly, taking the suitcase from my hand and hovering over me. He's just the perfect half a head taller than my five feet, seven inches. And his dark eyes are filled with fire. He looks deeply into my eyes, his warm breath making me dizzy.

"You realize that's what makes it so much fun, right?" he asks lowly. With a wink, he pulls away and neatly seats my suitcase in his open trunk, right next to his own.

And I do realize that he's right. This is hands-down one of the craziest and most exciting things I've ever done. And that's saying something.

As we slide into the car, he looks over at me. "You have a passport, right?"

I fish it out of my purse and wave it in the air at him.

"Good," he says, grinning. "Let's go."

As we drive, I pepper him with questions about the trip. I learn he's meeting a dozen or so friends, one of whom shares a house there, so there may be some bunking up, or I can always stay in a hotel. There will be no need to arrange additional transportation, as they're meeting in Naples and driving from there. And they'll be there a few weeks.

A few weeks in paradise. The more he talks, the better it sounds.

"You needn't stay the whole time," he assures me.

I wave a hand dismissively. "Spontaneous, remember? Let's get there and see what happens."

"If that's what you wish. But please don't do anything that could jeopardize your job on my account."

"They won't fire me," I assure him. "I work in a music store. They're all a bunch of flakes, and they're used to people pulling shit like this. Besides, it's not like I need the money anyway." I look out the window to hide the flush in my cheeks. I hadn't intended to say that last part.

"There's no shame in having money," he assures me, resting his hand briefly on my knee. "That you continue to work anyway says you're not content to waste your days shopping and tanning."

Shaken from my pity party, I turn to him and laugh. "Isn't that exactly what we're about to do?" I point out.

He smiles and shakes his head. "When you do it a little while, it's a holiday. When you do it all the time, it's a lifestyle. Big difference." He lets that sink in but continues on when I make no reply. "What instrument do you play?"

I almost give him a hard time for assuming I play an instrument because I work at a music store. But he's called me out on that kind of bullshit once already, and the man *is* taking me to Italy.

"Mandolin, mostly. But I've taught myself a little of everything — guitar, banjo, lute, ukulele…" I pause, willing myself to open up. "And I sing."

He smiles over at me. "Are you any good?" I blush so deeply he laughs. "Okay, maybe you can just show me sometime and I'll be the judge."

"You're a devious bastard," I tease.

He waggles an eyebrow as he pulls into the airport parking structure.

"You have no idea," he murmurs.

He's right. But I can't wait to find out.

We get our luggage out and head inside. The first leg of Alessandro's itinerary is to Paris. There are no coach seats left, but there are two first class seats. He doesn't hesitate to upgrade, so I don't hesitate to go for it. The flight from Paris to Naples has available seats, though apart, but it's short, and getting a break from each other at that point might not be the worst thing.

With that settled, we make our way through security.

As soon as we're through, something occurs to me, and I stop Alessandro with a sharp tug.

"Are Sera and my brother on our flights?" I can't keep the note of panic out of my voice. Because deciding to do something my brother would be upset about and flaunting it in his face are two very different things.

"No," he assures me swiftly. "Serafina specifically told me she switched them to avoid that. They will fly into Firenze, then they'll be staying there and other places around the country, but not where we'll be."

I let out a deep breath. And I finally get excited. I'm going to Italy. Only having been out of the country to go to Canada, that's huge. Though our family was comfortable growing up, Mom and Dad didn't want us to be spoiled little rich kids, so most of our family trips were very modest. Disneyland, Yosemite, the Grand Canyon, that sort of thing.

While we wait to board, and after I've sent the necessary texts and emails to let Mom and work know I'll be traveling indefinitely, I ask Alessandro about growing up in Italy. He tells me a good deal about his country, his friends, and his family, but stops abruptly when he gets to his reasons for coming to the United States.

I lay a hand on his thigh. "It's okay," I assure him. "Sera gave me the highlights."

Alessandro grimaces. "Normally, I'd be unhappy about that, but I guess it's better that you know."

His words give me pause, because what I know about him isn't exactly roses and sunshine. Sera told me how he fled his family's pressure to use his talent at making money through real estate development so they could pay off mob debt. The same debt that eventually got them killed and almost killed Alessandro and Sera. But, while they both managed to avoid serious injury, it all ended with my brother in the hospital. That's some pretty heavy stuff, and it doesn't exactly help him where I'm concerned. Suddenly I kind of wish I didn't know all that about him. That we were simply two people who met, had an instant and intense attraction, and decided to run off together. Though I guess we are still that.

I examine his face as he rubs a finger under his chin. "You do that a lot," I tell him, pointing at his chin.

He smiles at me. "Yes, and you twirl your hair," he teases.

"I do not," I protest.

He points and I look down to see my hair wrapped around one of my fingers. We both burst out laughing.

We board shortly thereafter, and once we're settled I'm more than happy to have splurged on first class. Though when he starts asking questions about my life, it has me squirming. But considering the scales are pretty tipped, I try not to hold back too much.

When he learns my age, his eyebrows jump.

"What? I'm only two years younger than Sera," I point out self-consciously.

"True," he allows. "Though at times I swore Serafina must be older than I am. She can be so serious."

I shrug. "It's why she and I work as friends. There has to be balance in any relationship. If you're too alike, you'll drive each other nuts."

"Is that why your relationships haven't worked out?" he asks shrewdly.

I narrow my eyes. "Yes, as a matter of fact. How did you know that?"

He presses his lips together to suppress his smile. "Don't worry, Serafina hasn't told me anything about you," he replies. "You just seem like you bounce around a lot. If you weren't so grounded in your family, I imagine you would be a nomad, moving around the country whenever and wherever you want."

"Probably," I agree with a smile. "Why do I feel like you already know me so well?"

His answering smile is tender. "Because I'm afraid we're quite a lot alike."

I nod. "So we're doomed," I reply matter-of-factly.

Alessandro laughs. "I'm afraid so."

"Well, let's enjoy it while it lasts then," I say with an overly dramatic sigh.

He considers me for a while before responding. "I already am," he finally responds. "You remind me what it's like to want more, and I think we both needed to do something drastically different for a while."

His eyes are alight with the passion he used to describe himself earlier. It pulls at something inside of me, and I can hardly believe I'm sitting here, on my way to Italy, next to this impossibly gorgeous man who just twenty-four hours ago I had pegged as a selfish asshole. Which he may yet be, should the opportunity present itself. But I'm starting to realize that he's so much more complex than that.

We are alike in our changing moods. But I sense, also like me, Alessandro is loyal to those he cares about. And while I don't expect we'll come to care for each other that deeply, it makes him that much more attractive. Though I don't miss that he hasn't so much as kissed me, or the implication that it's my impulsiveness that inspired him to bring me along. Sure, he's flirted, but being just as big of a flirt, I know how empty that can be. Because I basically told the man I'd have sex with him, and he's done nothing about it.

If I were smarter that would reassure me. As it is, I can't help but feel a little disappointed. I push the feeling down, determined to enjoy myself no matter what this trip does or does not bring. To just appreciate the experience and go with the flow.

To that end, we spend a while longer getting to know each other. He's smart with a sharp wit, and is more of a balance between risk-taker and playing it safe than I am. But then, he outstrips me in both years and life experience. I can't decide if it's intimidating or sexy. But then, why can't it be both?

* * *

I must have drifted off, because the next thing I know Alessandro is nudging me awake.

"We've landed," he says softly.

"Holy shit," I cry, springing up. "We're in Paris?"

Alessandro laughs. "You sleep like the dead. And yes. Have you been before?"

I lean over him to look out the window. "No," I reply softly. "This is officially the first time I've been out of North America."

Alessandro catches my face, turning it toward him. "Then I'm sorry we won't have time to see Paris. It's quite beautiful," he says softly, and in a way that makes me feel like it's not just Paris he's talking about.

"Some other time," I say without thinking.

A small smile flits across his face. "Some other time."

We collect our things and make the transition to our next flight seamlessly. And this time when we land, I'm wide awake. I can't drink in the sights around me fast enough.

As we take a taxi to the meeting point, I'm bouncing in my seat with anticipation. I barely have time to soak any of it in when we're out of the car and Alessandro is jumping into a hug with a huge group of people.

For a few minutes there's simply a lot of gesticulating, shouting, and back-clapping embraces. Amid the chaos I count eight men and three women. Two of the three women are clearly attached to men in the group. The third, not so much, at least not based on the looks and touches she gives Alessandro as they greet each other. It annoys me immediately. While I'm still not sure if anything would happen between us, I'm not that girl who competes for a man's attentions.

Before I can think too much more about it, Alessandro pulls me into the fold and introduces me. I'm horrible with names as it is, but I know I'll never remember all of them. Except her. Valentina. She's gorgeous in a way I'll never be, curved and feminine in all the places I'm flat and lacking. Being "willowy" has never made me so self-conscious.

We pile into three tiny cars. Alessandro sits beside me, rubbing my leg reassuringly.

"Will you all speak Italian the whole time?" I ask quietly.

He smiles so widely it crinkles the corners of his eyes. "*Mi dispiace,*" he says. "I'm sorry. But yes, they probably will."

I smile vaguely. "Oh, well, I'm sure I'll be fine," I murmur.

He leans close. "Don't worry, they all can speak English. I've asked them to try to remember to speak it around you as much as possible." He kisses me on the forehead.

On.

The.

Fucking.

Forehead.

Bryce kisses me on the forehead. My grandpa kisses me on the forehead. Instantly, my mood flips.

"So, you and Valentina," I spit out. His eyebrows fly up at my asinine tone. "You dated? Dating? Or is she another wife you conveniently forgot to mention?"

The guy in the front passenger seat shoots a look back at Alessandro. His jaw tightens, and he shakes his head at me and looks away. I've clearly insulted him. I should be sorry for reminding him about the estranged wife he hid from Sera while they were dating, as it's so far in the past and had nothing to do with me, but I'm not.

So I spend my time looking out the window as darkness settles in. Thankfully, it's not a long drive.

When we get to the house where we'll be staying, I'm shown to a tiny room with one bed. At least I get my own room. I'm not left alone long when there's a knock on my door.

"Come in," I call.

Alessandro's lean frame appears in the door.

"We're leaving for dinner shortly, but I'd like if we could talk," he says quietly.

I gesture widely for him to go on. He enters, closing the door gently behind him, then settles next to me on the bed.

"Valentina and I have been together in that way, though many years ago," he admits bluntly. I cross my arms over my chest and look away. He sighs deeply. "But that's not what I'm here for."

"I'm an idiot," I say, laughing. "Do whatever you want, Alessandro. Fuck her silly if that's what you really want. That's what we're both about, right? Being spontaneous. Doing whoever and whatever we want." For the first time I admit to myself that the feeling I'd had when I saw them greeting each other, saw her obvious interest in him, was jealousy. I'm nothing to him, I know. And the short time we've had to get to know each other has barely made us friends. But I guess I didn't realize how one-sided the attraction between us is.

"It's not what I want," he says simply. "Now let's just go to dinner. Once we've had something to eat, we can come back here and sleep, and by tomorrow most of the jet lag will have passed, and we'll both be thinking more clearly."

I turn my head back to look at him. "What aren't you thinking clearly about?"

He looks hesitant. "Honestly? I may have made a mistake. I feel like…" he trails off, clearly unsure of how to say whatever it is he's trying to say, "…you're in a place of transition. And I don't want to take advantage of that."

I shake my head, furious, climbing off the end of the bed to avoid having to go directly around him. "I'm not a fucking kid," I retort. "I'm a grown woman, here of her own volition. But maybe I'm just a kid to you."

I consider that. How would I feel about dating a man as many years younger than me than I am younger than him? But the distance between eighteen and twenty-eight is so much more than twenty-eight to thirty-eight.

"I know you're not," he says before I can make it to the door. "Believe me, I know it." I spin around to see him staring at me. Really staring at me, as if he's trying to undress me with his eyes. "But maybe I'm not in the best headspace right now, either." The look on his face is so pained, so raw, it pains me too. And again, I'm reminded that we're probably more alike in some ways than I'd care to admit.

I tilt my head back and laugh toward the low ceiling. "You know what I usually do when I feel that way?" I ask. "I fuck someone I couldn't give a shit about. Just to feel something besides what I don't want to feel."

"I did that for a long time," he says. "It never worked out well."

I tip my head back down and look at him. "Well, then I guess there's always booze," I reply with a wobble in my voice.

He laughs, and rises from the bed, stopping in front of me. "Yes, there's always booze," he agrees. His hands rest on my shoulders, skimming down my arms, then back up until his hands settle on either side of my face. "But when I fuck you, *Cara Mia*, it will be because we both know it's right. Not because we can't stand thinking about what's wrong."

My stomach flips at the implication. Maybe it wasn't as one-sided as I thought.

"What about kissing me?" I ask, looking up at him defiantly.

"You just won't take no for an answer, will you?" he asks with a smile.

"No more than you would," I point out.

He runs a finger down my cheek. "You have a fire in you," he murmurs. "I know what that feels like. But there's no rush."

"Maybe. Maybe not. What if the world ends tomorrow and all we have is right now?" I say, half teasing, half wondering what his holdup is.

He shakes his head. "It's still not our time."

"What if I've got nothing to offer but right now?"

Alessandro looks at me sadly. "Do you really believe that?" He strokes my cheek with his thumb. "You have fire, you have strength, and you have everything to give. Don't ever sell yourself short for anyone. Especially not me." And with that he pulls away.

I want to argue. I want to convince him to kiss me, to take me, here, now. To live in the moment with me. I can't explain to him that I'm not selling myself short, I've just never been one to think about anything beyond today.

"Why did you bring me here?" I ask, closing my eyes.

I feel his hands slide into mine, and he pulls me to him, letting go so he can wrap his arms around me. It feels too good not to hold him too, so I wrap my arms under his and rest my head against his chest. The steady beat calms me.

"I don't know, I didn't think too much about it," he murmurs into my hair. "It just felt right."

I agree with him, but I hold back, already feeling exposed. "Well, it's a start." I take a step back. "Shall we?"

With a smile, he gestures for me to precede him out.

It turns out the house we're staying in is pretty far up the hill, so we walk in a loud, raucous group down to the closest bar to eat. The lot of them spend hours eating, talking, and drinking, and I do my best to keep up. Though exhausted, I learn one thing. It's practically impossible to get an Italian drunk. They drink more than I do, which is saying something, but they space it out, and eat enough to where it hardly seems to affect them. Though it might also be the jet lag that's causing the little I drink to hit me hard.

I look over at Alessandro, though, and he seems completely unaffected. I swoon backward into the booth we're sitting in, giving up trying to engage. Thankfully, Valentina sits on the other end the whole time, so at least I haven't had to contend with her flirting for his attention. She seems happy enough to flirt with the other half dozen available men. The tramp.

I hear my name being spoken amid the rapid Italian shooting around the table, then warm arms sliding under me.

"Time to go home, *Cara Mia*," Alessandro says, his deep voice rumbling in my ear. I look up, realizing my head is on his chest.

"I can walk," I murmur sleepily.

He laughs, and it makes me smile.

"Shhhh, *bella*," he hushes me. "I've got you."

Too tired to protest further, I surrender, my eyelids sliding shut.

Chapter 3 — Emily

I wake up with more arms than I should have. Looking down, the one over my waist is significantly hairier. I crane my neck backward and see Alessandro tucked behind me.

I roll over with a smile, noting the small windows are open, and I can hear shorebirds calling in the early morning sunshine. It's plenty warm in the room, and I'm still wearing the slinky dress I put on for Bryce and Sera's party.

I examine Alessandro's face for a moment. He looks more his age when he's asleep, without the smile he usually has, but he's no less handsome for it. I stop myself from kissing him, or even touching him, though I want to do both. And a whole hell of a lot more.

"Like what you see?" he asks without opening his eyes. It startles me so much I jump back a little. He laughs, finally opening his eyes. "*Mi dispiace*. I didn't mean to scare you."

I push on his chest. "Yes, you did."

His answering sideways grin makes me wish we were wearing fewer clothes. "You're right, I did." He lifts his wrist to look at his watch. "*Perfetto*. It's almost nine. By the time we get cleaned up, there will probably be breakfast still."

He sits up, swinging his legs over the bed and unbuttoning his shirt to reveal a black undershirt.

"Don't you have your own room?" I tease him, propping my head up on my elbow.

He looks back at me with a sexy smirk. "*Sì, bella*. But I underestimated how tired I was last night, and I fell asleep here before I could make it there," he explains.

I give him a skeptical look. "Is that so?"

He tosses his shirt onto a chair beside the bed and turns back to me fully. "Quit laying there looking so sexy," he murmurs, not answering me. "This question may be the death of me, but I trust you brought a bathing suit?"

I narrow my eyes at him. "I'm starting to think you're just a big flirt," I reply. "But yes, I did. A two-piece, if you must know."

He looks mildly insulted, laying a hand over his chest in mock indignation. "Me? A flirt? Such accusations," he grumbles, teasing me.

"There's a bathroom just outside in the hall if you'd like a shower. Then be ready in your suit. Preferably with something over it so I don't do anything untoward at the breakfast table."

I sit up, shaking my head. "See? There you go again with the flirting."

"It's not flirting if you're serious."

"Pfff. Says who?"

He grins. "Me." He winks at me.

I shove his chest a little as I climb by him off the bed. "You're impossible."

He grabs my waist before I can get away, dragging me into his embrace. This close, his smell is strong, as neither of us has showered in a while, but it's also overwhelmingly appealing, and as I look up at him, the intensity in his expression takes my breath away.

"So I've been told," he murmurs. His face dips toward mine, and my breath catches in my throat.

His nose gently touches mine, gliding up, then down again. His hot breath fills my senses, and breathing is still difficult. He's alluring in a way I've never experienced, intense yet somehow still playful, and the anticipation of his kiss is killing me.

I bring my hand to his face, stroking the coarse hair of his beard. A small sigh escapes him, and his mouth finds mine. His kiss is soft, sensual, and more polite than I'd like it to be. At least, at first. I slide my hand back into his hair, gripping it as he kisses me. His hands wrap around my back, and he pulls me completely against him, deepening the kiss.

Finally, his tongue pushes into my mouth, and I accept it eagerly. But just when it's getting really good, he pulls away.

"This is exactly why I knew better than to kiss you. Now I need a cold shower," he teases. He runs a thumb over my lip.

"Be careful, or you're going to get more than a cold shower," I caution him.

He laughs and stands up. "Fair enough," he replies. "When you're ready, follow the smell of coffee." And with a wink, he's gone.

I hurry through a shower, and dress quickly in a shamelessly skimpy pink bikini, covering it with a pair of cutoff jean shorts and a white tank top, finishing with a pair of flat, white strappy sandals. And then, just

28

as he told me to, I follow my nose to the bottom floor, joining everyone in the kitchen as they sip at coffees and argue loudly. Well, it sounds like arguing, anyway.

Alessandro sits on a packed couch, across from another one, and they're all talking animatedly. He looks me up and down and gives me a wink as I pass by. I stick my nose in the air and pretend I don't see him. But I can see his amused grin in my peripheral vision. As I get breakfast, I chat idly with one of the other women, who kindly reminds me that her name is Bianca. She seems to be closer to my age, and her husband, Lorenzo, grew up with Alessandro and his brother. Soon she's telling me all sorts of stories about the trouble they'd get into as teenagers. As if sensing his secrets are being spilled, Alessandro wanders over and inserts himself into the conversation.

"Don't believe a word she says," he tells me with a deadpan expression. "Enzo made up all kinds of shit to impress her."

Bianca laughs. "As if I couldn't tell the difference," she chides him.

Alessandro laughs and looks down at me. I'm struck by his easy charm among his friends. He slides an arm around my waist. "Having fun?" he asks lightly.

"Very much," I reply, looking up at him. Wishing he'd take me back upstairs and finish what he started. But I'm also excited to explore. "What are we doing today?"

He chuckles and looks back to Bianca. "Americans, always in a rush," he jokes.

She shrugs. "I'm tiring of all this talk myself. Let's get out of here." She rises, fishing around behind the counter we were sitting at and producing a bag. Wrapping it around her body, she yells at her husband from across the room.

"Enzo, *andiamo!*"

He yells something back that I don't understand, and everyone laughs. I look at Alessandro.

He leans into me, whispering into my ear, "He called her his beautiful, bitchy alarm clock." My eyebrows jump, and he chuckles. "It's their way." He looks down at my outfit. "By the way, you look beautiful."

I narrow my eyes at him. "I bet you say that to all the girls," I tease him. In his bright blue board shorts and black tank top, he looks like a magazine ad for beachwear. His toned arms are tan, as is the bit of well-muscled chest peeking out the top of his shirt. With a pair of designer sunglasses hanging casually from his top, he looks ready to go. "But you don't look so bad yourself."

He plants a kiss on top of my head, then pulls me along. We take our time meandering down the hill. I don't mind the slow pace, as it gives me time to take everything in. It feels surreal finally being someplace so different from Seattle, someplace I've always wanted to go like this with its packed, colorful buildings, cobblestone walkways, and balmy sunshine. I don't bother with the hat or sunglasses I brought in my bag, letting the rays hit my face, soaking up every bit of their warmth.

We spend most of the day lying on the beach, tossing a frisbee around, splashing in the water when we get too warm. After lunch, the women lay out to tan, but it really ends up as a nap. Late in the day, we wander back up the hill, a final workout to top off a day of exhausting sunshine and laziness.

We cycle through showers and donning more appropriate clothes to go out for dinner, then head out to an actual restaurant, where we spend the rest of the evening and into the small hours of the next day.

Much as the night before, the food, alcohol, and laughter flow freely. I find myself participating more, all the while sticking close to Alessandro. It's hypnotic watching him slip so easily between English and Italian, his easy grace and warmth making me comfortable and happy by his side. By the end of the night, when I've spent most of my time watching him, I realize I'm way more into him than I was even this morning. No way I'm going to settle for "whatever."

Once we're all back at the house, he offers to walk me to my bedroom door, and I'm practically giddy with anticipation. Thankfully, he follows me in, taking a seat in the chair next to the bed as I remove my sandals. I sink onto the bed, suppressing a frown.

"You're awfully far away," I say, patting the bed next to me.

He raises an eyebrow. "Did you have good day?"

"Yes," I reply. "You seemed to enjoy yourself."

"I did," he agrees, crossing his legs. "It's been a long time since I've felt this relaxed." He rubs his chin thoughtfully. "You fit beautifully into the group. I expected it to be…" he pauses, searching for the word.

"Awkward?" I supply.

"Yes," he agrees, leaning forward. "Awkward."

"Like right now."

He laughs. "Yes, something like that."

"So are you going to spill or what?" I ask bluntly, folding my arms over my chest to demonstrate my impatience.

He slips off the chair and takes a seat next to me, brushing my hair back behind my shoulders tenderly. "Do you always say exactly what's on your mind?"

"Yep. Do you always avoid saying what's on yours?"

He considers that with a smirk. "Not always. Just when I think it will get me in trouble."

I roll my eyes. "That's exactly when you *need* to speak up."

"Even if it might upset you?"

I shake my head. "Are you really that scared of hurting my feelings? Yes. I'd rather be upset and know, than sitting here wondering what the hell you're thinking."

"That's refreshing." He takes a deep breath. "I'm afraid of ruining this. I find you fascinating, *Cara Mia*. You seem to understand me so well. You're a little too observant at times, really. And then you just say exactly what you're thinking. It unbalances me. You unbalance me." He stares at me intently. I stare right back. "I've always jumped into romance, like you seem to want to do now. But this feels different."

"Can we not?" I ask. "Overanalyze this, I mean. You're different than anyone I've ever known too. And I never thought I'd be doing this, with you, here, so fast. But thinking too hard causes more problems than it solves, in my experience. Can't we just be whatever it is we feel like being?"

The silence that follows my words is painful. So much so, I can't stand it. And I'm not used to having to convince a man to be with me. With a shake of my head, I rise, going to my suitcase and pulling out a nightshirt.

"You're not going to need that."

I whirl in place to find he's standing behind me. The fire in his eyes answers the question that I'd asked, that had been lingering uncomfortably in the air. Finally. I drop the nightshirt and go into his arms just as he reaches for me.

31

This time when he kisses me there's nothing tender about it. His lips are demanding, consuming my answering kisses with a fiery passion that immediately sets my skin ablaze for him. He works his hands under my blush sundress, sliding them over my ass as he pulls me back toward the bed. I press him down until he's seated, mounting him as our mouths continue to work together, as I wrap my hands in his luscious hair. I pull at it hard, tipping his mouth away from mine.

"Do you have a condom?" I ask breathlessly. He nods. *Thank fucking God.* "Good. Now undress me."

"As you wish," he replies with a sultry smile. In one swift motion, he pulls the sundress over my head and discards it on the floor. His hands trace back down my chest, over my nude lace bra, down the matching thong. His fingers stroke me over the fabric, and I grip his shoulders as the hot fire of desire rises in me under his touch. His deft fingers reach around and undo my bra, and he discards it. His hands swirl over my breasts, pinching at my taut nipples, before tracing down my stomach. "You're stunning."

I look down at him. "And you're still dressed."

He slides me off his lap onto the bed, and wastes no time removing his clothes as I lay back against the pillows. "Better?" he asks, turning to me.

I slide a hand under my panties, stroking myself. I watch his sizeable cock harden as he takes it in. I lift my other hand, twirling my finger.

"Turn around."

He does so and I get a good look at his gorgeous ass. I slide off my panties and, unable to help myself, I sit up and run my hands over his rock-hard backside. Then I slip my arm around him, grabbing him and stroking firmly. His left hand reaches back and latches onto my arm. "Fuck."

"Condom?"

His right hand flicks up, the packet held between two fingers. I snatch it away from him, open it, and roll it over his hard length before turning him back around and pulling him onto the bed.

"What, no foreplay?" he teases.

I push him down onto the pillows and swing my leg over him, hovering above him. "We've had days of foreplay," I reply. "I need to fuck you before I go insane."

His head tips back slightly and his muscles tense. "God, yes," he breathes.

I reach between us, stroking him, lifting him into position. His throbbing tip grazes me and it takes everything I have to concentrate through these first few, sensitive touches. And as I slide him into me, I enjoy every goddamn inch of heat that licks through me. There's nothing so good as this moment. Well, not until the end anyway.

I look down at him, and I can feel the flush of my cheeks, the tightness of my nipples. He sees it, and reaches up, stroking and pulling at them. I shift gently, rocking him inside me. We both gasp at how good it feels. His hands drop to my hips, begging for more.

And I don't disappoint him. I rock slowly at first, until he's groaning beneath me, until I'm soaking wet enough to really ride him. Once I am, I lean into him, arching my hips to slide him in and out, faster, harder, until I feel my climax building. I sit up so he's fully buried in me and give myself a moment to watch his perfectly exquisite face contract with pleasure. Letting go, I grind into him, stimulating myself inside and out until my orgasm swirls inside me.

It's when the expletives start rolling off my tongue, and Alessandro grabs my nipples, pinching and pulling into my release. It sends the fire shooting between my core and my breasts and back again before exploding out into my limbs as I ride the wave of my climax. When I finally descend, I sink into him, a mewling, trembling mass of post-orgasmic bliss.

He shifts beneath me, holding me to him with one hand, using the other to hold my ass in place while he pushes up from the bed and continues to take me. I didn't expect it, and I gasp into the amazing feeling of him fucking me. But he can only go so deep from this angle. So, I roll to the side, and he rolls with me, pressing into me to stay inside.

He slips my legs up onto his shoulders, then braces against them, dragging my ass into his lap so he can take me hard and fast. Soon, my legs are trembling in anticipation of another orgasm. He drops one of my legs and presses into me, circling his hips when he's in to the hilt so he's rubbing against me with every thrust. I cry out, and he smirks down at me, knowing exactly what he's doing, how crazy it's making me. He slows, deliberately pulling all the way out, only to plunge back in fully again.

"Please," I beg.

"Shhhh," he responds. "Trust me."

And though I'm aching for release, I give myself to him. I surrender to his rhythm, allowing him to fill me only to leave me void over and over, slowly, torturously. Without warning, instead of burying his cock in me, he slips a hand between us, vigorously pumping into me. The switch-up has me arching off the bed, but before I can so much as gasp, his cock enters me once again and his mouth attaches to mine. Plunging his tongue in my mouth, he keeps his cock buried deep, rubbing in a way that brings me abruptly to the edge and hangs me there. My hands find his ass, holding on for dear life, encouraging him. His mouth drops to my neck, his heavy breathing tickling my ear.

I moan into him, and he moans back. I tilt my hips up, needing him as deep as he can go. It changes things just enough to tip me into climax, and I clench around him.

"Ohhhh, *mio dio*," he moans as his muscles tighten. "*Cazzo, sto venendo*." I can feel his orgasm shudder through him, and it turns me on so much it interrupts my descent, giving me one last jolt of pleasure.

As both of our bodies finally relax, he presses his forehead into my neck. It feels so good laying here with him still between my legs that I'm not ready to let go quite yet.

"What does, '*Cazzo, sto venendo*' mean?" I ask curiously, stroking his damp back.

Alessandro laughs. "Fuck, I'm coming." When I laugh too, he picks his head up to look me in the eyes and gives me a light kiss on the lips. "That was amazing."

"Mmm, yes, it was," I agree. "Teach me something else in Italian."

He leans back, pulling out, much to my dismay. After he's discarded the condom, he lays back down next to me.

"*Sei il miglior fra tutti quelli che mi sia mai scopate*," he says slowly.

I laugh but let him repeat it to me until I can repeat it back.

"*Sei il miglior fra tutti quelli che mi sia mai scopate*," I'm finally able to say. "What does it mean?"

He's unable to suppress his shit-eating grin. "It means, 'You're the best fuck I've ever had,'" he replies, bursting into laughter.

I pull the pillow from behind my head, rise to my knees, and proceed to whack him with it. "You arrogant bastard," I cry out. "I can't believe you seriously just made me tell you that." I continue beating him with the pillow as he laughs. I give him one, final hard whack in the face. "Honestly." I try to throw as much disgust into the word as I can, but I'm having a hard time not laughing.

He pulls the pillow away from me and puts it behind his head. "Maybe I was telling you you're the best fuck *I've* ever had," he replies.

"Maybe?"

"Or maybe not." He laughs again, acknowledging that I'm clearly not falling for it. "Am I?"

I narrow my eyes at him. "Maybe," I reply airily. "Teach me something else."

"Hmmm. Perhaps I need to teach you something that will help you answer my question," he says suggestively. I laugh, and gesture for him to continue. "*Leccamela tutta.*"

"That's much less of a mouthful," I remark. He bursts out laughing. "What?"

He shakes his head, wiping tears of laughter from his eyes. When he's regained composure, he looks at me, trying to keep the laughter at bay. "Just say it," he urges. "I promise you won't regret it. *Leccamela tutta.*"

I give him a stern look, not sure if he's trying to fool me. "*Leccamela tutta,*" I say.

An evil glint appears in his eyes and he prowls toward me. I don't flinch or move an inch. He pries open my naked legs, pushing me back onto the pillows. Then his head disappears, and I feel his tongue *there.*

"Holy shit," I gasp, realizing what he had me ask him to do. But as his tongue laps at the extra-sensitive folds between my legs, my brain fogs and heat builds in me, and I find I'm not able to protest. Scratch that, I don't want to.

While he sucks and nibbles at my nub, sending me into a trembling frenzy, his beard tickles my opening, his chin pressing into my sex in a way that has me wetter than I ever remember being. The erotic sounds of him lapping at me are unbelievable. In a slow build, he caresses me in ways I'd never dreamed of, and though I could languish in the amazing feeling forever, I'm soon coming on his face, whimpering my release, too overwhelmed to do anything else.

He sits up, looking extremely satisfied with himself. And damn well he should be. He wipes his face, removing as much of the moisture from his beard as he can.

"Well?" he teases.

I nod in defeat. "*Sei il miglior fra tutti quelli che mi sia mai scopate.*" He beams with pride. "You should teach classes on what you just did there."

He laughs, sliding down next to me. "I don't do that for just anyone, you know."

"Oh, so I'm special?" I tease back, turning toward him and running my hands down his chest.

He strokes my face, kissing me gently. "More than you know," he says seriously.

"And you were the best I've had even before the mind-blowing oral," I reply.

He lunges for my mouth with his, capturing my bottom lip between his teeth before plunging his tongue into my mouth. I wasn't expecting the intensity, but I'm finding the feeling of his mouth on any part of me to be very addicting, so I sure as hell don't mind.

We sleep together that night, wrapped around each other peacefully. As it happens, it's also the best sleep I've ever had.

Chapter 4 — Emily

On Wednesday morning, I wake nestled in the corner against the wall. I try to wriggle upright only to bump into Alessandro, who is spread-eagled in the small bed, taking up ninety percent of its surface.

I shake my head and start pushing him out of bed. What a pig. I decide a good, solid fall to the floor will be a fitting punishment. But he's heavier than he looks, being all lean muscle, and he starts to wake up before I can get him over the edge.

He grabs at me, rolling me onto my back. "That's not very nice," he chastises me, pinning me beneath him.

I wriggle violently. "Yeah, well, it's not nice to hog the bed, either," I reply, sticking my tongue out at him.

With a grin, he descends upon it, covering my mouth with his and joining his tongue to mine. Suddenly, I'm less mad and more horny. Noting with satisfaction that he's got morning wood, I twist suddenly and give a swipe of my leg to topple him onto the bed. Thankfully, he left his stash of condoms on the nightstand, so I grab one and suit him up before climbing on top of him. Unsurprisingly, he doesn't protest, watching me with amusement.

Until I sink down on him. Then he's throwing his head back in pleasure. And it feels pretty damn good for me too. I take my time riding him, testing to see what we both like best. He's being lazy this time around, letting me take control, simply watching me with his arms tucked behind his head. I have to say it's a pretty big turn-on.

The more intently he watches, the more turned on I get. I close my eyes, still feeling his on me, and I surrender to the moment. I work my nipples, then rub myself between my legs as I bounce over him. A few hard circles on my clit, and I'm groaning as I start to come. His hands find my hips, helping keep the pace as I languish in the orgasm, barely able to move while I explode in ecstasy. He gives a few ferocious thrusts and a groan that tells me he's finished too.

I sink onto him with a catlike grin.

"Good morning," I purr.

"Fucking amazing morning," he replies, kissing me deeply. "Let's just stay here and do this all day."

I laugh. "No dice, sir. I've had a taste of real Italian food, and there's none in this bed, so you're out of luck."

He laughs loudly. "Not even two full days in Italia and you're already spoiled," he teases.

I smirk at him and climb off of his gorgeous body, stretching widely. "I'm going to take a shower," I proclaim. He sits up on his elbows and raises an eyebrow suggestively. "*Alone.* I'd like to eat before noon."

With a sigh, he climbs to his feet and starts to dress. "If we must," he replies. He's dressed quickly and, with a smack on my ass and a kiss on my cheek, he leaves me to get ready.

I can't keep the smile off my face the whole time, either. Being with him definitely puts me in a good mood. Or maybe it's the setting. Or being on vacation. Bah, who knows, and who cares? I'm going to enjoy every damn minute of it.

As I descend into the main area, the smell of pastries is overwhelming, and my mouth starts to water.

"Ohhhh, who is my new best friend?" I joke as I step off the stairs.

Valentina looks up from the freshly opened bakery box she's obviously just set out and puts her hands on her hips.

"Ah. Never mind," I mutter. But as soon as she's taken one and wandered off, I sneak my own. I find the farthest seat from her and descend upon the delicious smelling pastry gleefully.

It's how Alessandro finds me minutes later, though it's almost gone, and I'm covered in chocolate glaze.

"You look like a chipmunk," he teases me, setting down two cups of coffee.

I chew quickly and swallow, grabbing at the cup nearest me and drinking greedily.

"Thank you," I reply earnestly.

"For calling you a chipmunk?" he asks with a confused look.

I roll my eyes. "For the coffee, dummy."

"Oh, I'm a dummy now, am I?" he asks.

I give him a stern look. "If I'm a chipmunk, you're definitely a dummy."

He shakes his head and laughs. "Fair enough," he agrees. "But finish quickly. We're leaving soon."

"Ooh, where to?" I ask eagerly.

"Driving a bit up the coast to spend the day at a different beach. But same plan. Lounging. Eating. Trying to sneak away to make love to you in the ocean," he says nonchalantly.

I wrinkle my nose at him. "We didn't do that last one yesterday."

He finishes his coffee, rises, and leans in to kiss me on the cheek. "Then we have some catching up to do," he murmurs into my ear.

Shivers shoot down my spine. I bolt down the rest of my food and follow him as fast as I can. Screw looking too eager. It's going to be a damn good day.

* * *

It turns out to be an understatement. The drive is so ridiculously beautiful, I'm practically crying by the time we get to our destination. And we spend the rest of the morning and into the afternoon lounging by the shore, playing in the water, and generally just enjoying the crap out of ourselves. After lunch, we return to the beach, where we vie for spots under umbrellas or in the shade to nap off the food coma. But it was totally worth it.

Alas, before I can drift off, Alessandro is tugging at my hand.

"Come," he urges quietly. I let him pull me up, and we walk quietly, hand in hand, down to the water's edge and along the shore.

Before long we pass a group of rocks. Alessandro pulls me between them, and we nestle into the soft sand, him leaning against a smooth rock, me leaning against his chest.

"If you brought me here to have sex, you're going to be very disappointed," I say softly. "I don't fancy getting sand in my private parts."

He laughs lowly. "No, *Cara Mia*. I just wanted you to myself for a while."

I turn my head to look up at him, and he lightly skims my lips with his.

"Tell me about your music," he prompts.

I huff a small laugh. "That's a pretty broad question," I hedge.

He shrugs, running his hands up and down my arms soothingly. "Okay," he allows. "What was the first instrument you learned to play?"

The memory so forcefully pops into my head, I can't help but smile. "Piano. My dad started teaching me when I was six." A pang of longing shoots through me.

"You miss him," Alessandro murmurs. I turn and look at him in shock. He squeezes my shoulders. "I could feel it. Here. And I can hear it in your voice."

"I do," I admit. "I try not to think about it much. He and I were so much alike." I shake my head.

"Was that a bad thing?" he asks.

I tuck my legs under me, playing with the hem of his board shorts. "Sometimes. But most of the time we just had a lot of fun together. Mom and Bryce are the serious ones. They thought we were nuts."

"You are a little nuts," Alessandro replies, smiling. "But in a good way. Mostly."

I turn and poke him in the stomach. "Be careful," I warn him. "I assume you still want to get laid later."

He puts his hands up in surrender.

"You know, music is one of my great loves as well," he admits.

"Oh, really?" I ask skeptically.

"Nothing can move me like a good piece of music," he asserts. "Though I'm hopelessly lacking musical talent. But I admire those with it greatly."

I shrug. "It's not a big deal. I'm sure there are things you're better at. You know. Real estate stuff."

He laughs loudly. "Yes, real estate stuff. I'm quite good at that."

"You're good at other things too," I remind him with a suggestive grin.

"Mmmm," he replies, his eyes locking on mine. "Are you asking for a demonstration?" His voice is thick with desire, and just the sound of it turns me on.

"Maybe," I whisper hoarsely.

He turns me back around so I'm against his chest, running his hands over my breasts, baring them to the warm air. His thumbs prime my nipples as his mouth runs along the shell of my ear, his hot breath unbearably sexy against my skin. One hand drifts down, skimming my stomach, slipping under my bikini bottoms. His fingers slip between my folds, stroking me gently at first.

"*Cara Mia*," he whispers in my ear. "You are unbelievably sexy." I moan into the stimulation. "Yes, let me hear you." His deft fingers stroke and slide, and I'm writhing in his arms. My hands go to his thighs, holding on for dear life as he rubs me into a frenzy. I try to keep the volume down, but I just know when I come, I'm going to scream.

He seems to know it too, because a moment before, he turns my head with his free hand, and my moans erupt into his mouth, muffling the sound.

As I drift back down to earth, he wraps his arms and legs around me. Once I've fixed my top, we settle in and watch the surf lap at the shore for a while longer. And when he unwraps himself, stands, and offers me a hand, I just stare. Because I want to etch this moment in my memory. I can't remember ever being quite this happy. And I know it won't last forever. It never does.

We rejoin our group just in time for the last round of post-nap beach antics before dinner. Dinner is, as usual, an all-night affair of eating, drinking, and talking. After which we drive home, and Alessandro and I have sex in the shower, then spend the last of our waking moments talking about everything and nothing.

He continues to amaze me with his ability to listen, share himself completely, and make me feel like I can tell him anything. And the fact that he's beyond amazing in bed doesn't hurt, either. As we drift peacefully to sleep after going at it one final time, I can't help but think to myself that this is like living in a fairy tale. And I'm already dreading the day I have to go back to reality.

* * *

The next day is much of the same, just a different beach, a different lunch spot. But for dinner, Alessandro steers me away as the others head to a nearby restaurant.

"I have something special planned, *Cara Mia*," he tells me with an excited grin.

"Oh? Is this the part where you finally get me alone and I find out you're really an ax murderer?" Just to be weird, I say it like I'm excited about it, and he gives me an impatient look.

"Yes," he deadpans. "You caught me." He rolls his eyes. "No, crazy. Come, I'll just show you."

He takes me by the hand and leads me away from the main tourist area, meandering up a side street that looks like it goes up a hill to nowhere. But as we turn the final corner, I'm surprised to find an old, towering restaurant tucked away on a cliff.

He gestures to the entrance. "If you think you love Italian food now, you're going to be in heaven soon," he explains. "Trust me."

I give him a look somewhere between surprised and sad. "You're too sweet to me."

He stops, a frown pulling at the corners of his mouth. Getting up in my face, he lifts my chin. "You deserve it," he tells me seriously, looking deeply into my eyes. "Don't ever doubt that."

I want to tell him I don't, but I don't want to argue and spoil his wonderful surprise. "Thank you," I reply sincerely. "For bringing me here. Now quit being so cute and feed me."

He laughs lightly but stays to kiss me for a moment before leading me inside.

And by the time we're done eating hours later, I couldn't argue with him if I wanted to. I'm too blissed out over the most amazing meal of my life. With the most amazing views. With an amazing man, whom I still can't reconcile with the selfish ass I'd pegged him as. I don't consider myself particularly romantic, but dinner with him was off-the-charts intimate.

As we walk home, I say the first prayer I've said in years that he's really this man. That I was wrong about him before, when all I had to go on was what someone else told me. But deep down, I have trouble believing it. It's so much easier believing the bad things.

Not even another night of amazing sex completely wipes away my fears. Because the better this gets, the more I keep expecting it to all come crashing down.

* * *

The next day, Friday, Bianca decides we're going to have a bonfire that evening. It's a slapped-together affair of convenience store food, which is still leaps and bounds better than the American kind, straight-up bottles of booze, and a few stray games and instruments they're able to find. So that night we do indeed find ourselves by a moderately large fire, though the night is still quite warm. It means, at least, I didn't have to change out of my bikini, shorts, and tank that have become my vacation uniform.

Seated on a blanket just outside of the main ring around the fire, I stretch my legs out and am considering how tan they've gotten in such a short time when Alessandro approaches with a guitar in hand.

"It's the best I could do. Will you play for me?" he asks.

I take it from him, weighing the acoustic in my hands. I check that it's in tune and strum a few chords.

"Couldn't hurt, I guess. Any requests?"

He leans down to kiss me on the cheek and then stretches out on the blanket to watch. "Whatever makes you happy," he replies huskily. I stare at him for a moment, his face in shadow, the light of the fire flickering against his back. I let the moment flow through me, sink in deep, and then I let it out through my fingers.

I close my eyes, surrendering myself to the music, not even sure exactly what I'm playing, but still hearing the music pouring out of the old instrument, nonetheless.

As I finish the first song, I open my eyes. Everyone has settled themselves near us, intently listening to me play. I finish and give a laugh when they all start clapping enthusiastically.

There are various calls of *"Bravissima!"* and "More!" but I note Alessandro still lays on his side, staring at me, the fire now in his eyes. I know without a doubt that if we were alone, he'd be taking me on this blanket right now. I play more, but as far as I'm concerned, he's my only audience. He doesn't take his eyes off me as I continue playing a second, third, then a fourth song. Finally, my out-of-practice fingers need a break, and I thank everyone graciously for their applause.

I set the instrument gently down on the blanket next to me, and they all go back to what they were doing. Alessandro rises, offering me a hand.

"Walk with me?"

I take his hand without a word, and he leads me down the beach. We stop at a group of benches, settling in on one to watch the gentle lapping of the water at the shore.

"You play beautifully," he says softly.

"Thank you," I reply simply.

"Will I ever get to hear you sing?"

I look over at him in horror. "No. Um, decidedly not."

He frowns. "Surely, it can't be that bad."

I shrug. "It's not that. Singing in front of people is a level of vulnerable I'm just not ready for." I have to stop myself from saying "I'm not capable of." That would be a little too much honesty.

Thankfully, he lets it drop, and we sit, starting out at the dark water.

"I don't want this to ever end," I say softly.

He stares stoically at the ocean. "But it will," he assures me softly.

"And then what?"

I make a noise of frustration and shake my head. "That's a question for another day."

He turns and catches my eye. "I'm asking now."

"No, you're treading into dangerous territory now."

"Nonetheless, I'm curious."

I heave a deep sigh. "I don't know," I reply honestly. "I guess we just keep going and see what happens."

"Is that what you want?" he asks plainly, turning toward me and pulling at the hem of my shorts.

"Yes," I say. "For now."

I didn't mean to say the last part and I can see it's not sitting well with him.

"So this is more a vacation fling for you?" he asks, hurt in his voice.

"Why are you suddenly so worried about this?" I ask.

"Because I found out today that I need to go back to Seattle on Sunday. My company needs me. And you're welcome to stay, but I want to see you once we're home. Though it doesn't sound like you feel the same," he replies genuinely.

"I'm surprised you do," I admit. "I figured this was just a vacation fling for you too. Surely you don't really want to piss my brother off. Or Sera. I'm not sure she'd be okay with this, either."

"I think Serafina would be happy for us," he responds. And though I'd never admit it, he's probably right. "And I thought you weren't worried about what the giant thought anymore."

"When he's not here to care, no." But it's so much more than that. I can feel myself fighting being with him. Still, my brother is the first and most obvious reason this just won't work.

Though it clearly was the wrong thing to say. Alessandro rises, fuming, and folds his arms over his chest. "Not wanting a relationship is one thing, but I didn't sign up to be your dirty secret, either."

"Oh, please, you're not my dirty secret, don't be so dramatic," I snap, rising to my feet as well.

Alessandro barks a laugh and runs a finger under his chin, clearly agitated. "Coming from you, that's ironic," he retorts. "Everything is drama with you. I can't even tell you I want to date you without you getting upset."

And just like that, I'm seeing red. I whirl on my heel, stomping away.

"Dammit, Emily, come back," he demands. But I don't listen. I stomp up the beach as he follows. The Alessandro of legend is finally making an appearance.

"Fuck off, Alessandro," I bark back at him.

He jogs up beside me, putting himself in my path.

"I won't," he says obstinately.

"You want to see drama? I'll give you drama," I spit at him. "I shouldn't have come here with you. My opinion of you before we met was dead-on, I just let your stupid fucking charm cloud my judgment. God, I should know better by now. I always date the same jerks, just with an accent this time. News flash: you don't get to make demands from me and then tell me who I am."

He throws his hands up in the air and I flinch away, my guard momentarily down. "Fine. You want to throw a temper tantrum? Be my guest." He steps aside, and I scurry off as fast as I can, away from his wrath, away from him, my heart pounding in my chest.

The arduous walk back to the house doesn't do much to cool me off. When I get back to my room, I pace around until I hear everyone returning. It's still early, so I hear them settle in downstairs to chat and, presumably, drink in the living room. I stop pacing, not wanting to draw attention to myself. Sitting on the bed quietly goes a long way toward calming me down, finally. And once I do, I'm able to admit to myself that I may have overreacted a little. But he's still got some apologizing to do too.

I trudge downstairs and peek into the living room, but there's not even half a dozen people there, and he's not among them. Assuming he's gone to bed, I head to his room.

I knock once, and nobody answers, but there's clearly a light coming from under the door. So I knock again.

"Alessandro, it's me. Please, I know you're angry, but we need to talk," I say through the door.

I hear shuffling, then, "We're busy, fuck off little girl." The voice is unmistakably a woman. And not just any woman. Valentina.

My heart drops, and I turn on my heel and run back to my room. Thankful that almost everything is still in my suitcase, I pack even faster than when I did to run here with Alessandro. Because now it's time to run away.

I flee back down the stairs in time to see Alessandro standing at his door down the hallway, looking at me in terror, realizing that I'm leaving.

"I hope she was worth it," I spit at him. But I don't wait for a response, I just keep going. Predictably, he follows.

"Can you please stop and talk to me?" he calls.

"No," I call back over my shoulder as I fly out the front door. "Why don't you go back and talk to your girlfriend?"

"Emily," he calls. "Ow!" I look back, and he's holding a bare foot in his hands, pulling something out of it. Good. I hope he really hurt himself.

Practically blind with the tears I hadn't realized I'd started shedding, I flee down the hill, looking for a place to hide and call a taxi. It's time to go home.

Chapter 5 — Serafina

Two weeks later

"Hey, baby?" Bryce's head peeks around the stairs. I look up from my book.

"What's up?" I prompt, setting the novel down on the coffee table next to me.

The rest of him comes into view and, as usual, the sight of him still makes my heart race a little. My husband. Even the thought makes me want to throw him down on the couch and do naughty things to every inch of his gorgeous body. And that's a lot of inches. In every respect.

He stops at the foot of the couch, giving me the same admiring look I'm sure I'm giving him.

"Damn, you look good there," his deep voice rumbles, glancing at the stack of books on the floor next to me and the pile on the coffee table. "Like a sexy little librarian." His blue eyes sparkle mischievously, and I know he's thinking about doing naughty things to me too. And here I thought once the honeymoon was over, we'd be tired of going at it like rabbits.

"Thanks," I reply. "But what were you going to ask me?"

"Oh, right," he replies, his trademark sunshine smile splitting his face. "Have you talked to my sister since we got back?"

"No, why?"

He sinks onto the couch next to me, pulling my legs into his lap and stretching his out on the coffee table while he rubs lazy circles into the bottom of my foot with his strong hands. "Mom called. She hasn't heard from her since she got back from her trip."

"Mmmm," I reply, distracted by the foot massage. "Wait. Emily was on a trip?"

Bryce drops my foot and smacks himself in the head. "That's right, I forgot. Damn. I got a voicemail from Mom the day after we left. She mentioned Emily had taken off after the party on some last-minute vacation. I meant to tell you, but, well, you know..." He grins at me suggestively.

"Yes, you were more focused on taking me on every surface of our hotel room," I murmur. I'm sure Italy is gorgeous, but frankly we mostly only ended up seeing the inside of our hotel rooms. For two whole weeks. Except the gelato. I made sure we escaped for that at least once a day.

He runs a hand forcefully over his short, chestnut hair, and I know exactly what kind of agitated he is right now. My whole body starts to tingle in response, but I shove it down and try to focus. We really need to learn to be able to have full, normal conversations again at some point.

"So where'd she go?"

He shakes his head. "Don't know. She didn't say, and nobody has talked to her."

"I'd say that's out of character for her, but—"

"But it's not," he agrees. "Yeah. I'm more worried about why. I hope our getting married didn't have anything to do with it."

I can't help the look of surprise on my face. "Surely she would've said something. I mean, Allie was pissed too, and she sure let us know. Emily's never really been the type to hold back with me."

He shakes his head, a small frown tugging at his mouth. "Em's fine calling people out on their shit. But if it's anything serious going on with her, she closes up tighter than a camel's ass in a sandstorm."

"Bryce!" I reach out and smack him on the arm as hard as I can.

He laughs. "What?"

I shake my head at him. "Whatever. Should we be worried?"

"Nah, I'm sure she'll turn up when she's ready to talk," he assures me. He gives me a look and stills. "But you should be worried. That little smack you just gave me woke The Beast."

I press my lips together to suppress a laugh. "I'm still not going to start calling it that."

He turns toward me and climbs between my legs, hovering over me. "Oh, it'll rub off on you eventually."

"Pun intended?" I tease.

With a grin, he leans in and covers my mouth with his, wasting no time feeling me up under the grey shirtdress I'm wearing. I run my hands over his muscled arms, gently stroking his tongue with mine, waiting for him to realize what *isn't* under my clothes.

He gasps and pulls away. "Dirty girl," he whispers as his hand slides between my legs unhindered by the panties that aren't there.

"Please," I say into his mouth. "You know you like it." I grab his semi-hard cock through his sweat pants. "And I'd bet anything you're not wearing underwear, either."

"Baby, I'd walk around naked if you'd let me, just so I could fuck you silly the instant you wanted me."

I suck a sharp breath in through my teeth. "You sure know how to distract a girl." I lift my foot and use it to press against his massive chest until he's a safe distance away. But I'm sure it gives him a full display of what's under my dress, because he can't tear his eyes away. "Strip, Hoyt."

"Anything you say, Mrs. Hoyt." He hooks his thumbs into his white T-shirt and removes it in a flash. The sight of his chiseled chest and abs never gets old. A second later he kicks off his grey sweats, freeing his massive cock. And I have to admit, The Beast is a pretty appropriate name for it. Impressively huge and as insatiable as he is, it's definitely one of my favorites of his body parts.

"I'm so glad we decided to stay home this weekend," I murmur. Then, before he can respond, I lean forward and take him in my mouth, slowly teasing him. As usual, the noises he makes leaves me slick and ready. And when he enters me, I can barely stand how much he fills me, how I never seem to completely adjust to his size. And I'm glad for it.

But he goes slow, torturing me. I hook my leg around his backside, urging him to go faster, deeper. He grins and shakes his head.

"Always so impatient." He reaches down and strokes my breasts, then slips his hands under my hips. In a flash, he's holding me tightly by them and pounding into me so hard I think my building orgasm has its own orgasm before I eventually shatter into pieces.

When we've cleaned up, and the need to be wrapped in each other has subsided once more, or at least for the next hour or two, I pick up my phone and try to call Emily. But it goes straight to voicemail. I leave her a generic message, asking her to give me a call, but as soon as I hang up, something starts niggling at the back of my mind.

Bryce is now settled on the other end of the couch with his own book, and he looks up as I struggle to remember whatever it is I've forgotten.

"Everything okay?" he asks softly.

I shake my head. "I feel like there's something about Emily I should be remembering."

He closes his book on a finger to keep his place. "Did she say something about taking off before we left?"

I shake my head. "Not that I can remember." The harder I try to remember, the less defined the thought becomes.

"Don't worry, I'm sure she'll call one of us back soon. She just does this sometimes. Usually because of a guy. It's why I didn't try to figure out where she went. I didn't want to have to kill anyone," Bryce jokes.

And like lightning hits, I remember in a flash. I barely keep the words "Oh, fuck" from tumbling out of my mouth. Because while I don't know if Emily was still seeing the guy she'd been casually dating, I'm pretty sure she didn't care enough about him to be all that upset if they had broken up. But I do remember who she was flirting with at our engagement-turned-wedding party. Alessandro fucking Giordano. And that he was still supposed to be leaving that same night for his Amalfi Coast vacation.

"Right," I reply with an affected smile before I can freak out too badly. "Wouldn't want that."

Bryce goes back to his book, seemingly clueless as to the thoughts racing through my head. A million questions go through my mind. Alessandro wouldn't really pursue Bryce's sister, would he? And even if he did, he's not so impulsive as to try to whisk her off to Italy with him, is he? I don't even need to ask myself if Emily is impulsive enough to go with him. She totally is. Or if she'd find him attractive — she's got eyeballs. And damned if he isn't charming when he wants to be.

But I also remember her being the one to force me to admit last year that his selfishness was what was keeping our relationship from working. But then, I can't say I've ever heard of Emily dating a guy for all that long, much less being in a relationship. So maybe looking for a guy who's actually relationship material isn't that high on her list. Or maybe, just like I once did, she saw him as an opportunity for some no-strings-attached fun.

Shit. The truth of it slams into me. But before I can jump to conclusions, I work on settling myself. Because if I panic, Bryce's finely tuned radar will go off. And if it really is true…

I shudder lightly, pushing down the thought. One thing at a time. Alessandro is still my friend. Having been through so much together, we'll always have a unique bond. One that works better if my husband doesn't kill him.

As casually as I can, I pick up my phone and text Alessandro. Since Emily is clearly shutting everyone out, I highly doubt she's going to call me back. But Alessandro wouldn't dare lie to me again. I hope.

* * *

Alessandro is a bit more difficult to pin down than usual, but he eventually agrees to meet me for lunch on Wednesday. Since Emily is also still silent, both Bryce and his mother have tried her at her apartment, with no answer. Bryce even goes down to the music store she works at, only to find out she's quit. Thankfully, Bryce has been busy running his family's corporate security company, and I manage to keep my suspicions under wraps, though it requires a lot of distraction. Mostly the kind of thing we would've already been doing, so it's not a difficult line to walk. But it's only a matter of time before Bryce decides to find out where Emily went that week, and with whom, hoping to shake loose answers that will help him get her to contact him or their mother.

So I'm itching for answers by the time Alessandro shows up and joins me at the private booth I've secured at my favorite seafood restaurant.

As he approaches, I note from afar that he looks just the same as always, well-coifed in a dark grey suit and black button-front shirt open at the collar, his dark hair and beard styled perfectly. But as he gets closer, I can see it in his eyes. Hurt.

Still, he greets me warmly, with a hug and a kiss on the cheek. "Serafina," he says. "You're glowing. I see marriage agrees with you."

I give him a guarded smile and take my seat, while he takes his opposite me. "Thank you," I reply. "It does, very much. How are you?"

I can see him suppress a sigh as he fixes me with his usual sideways smile. But it has none of its usual charm.

"Work has been stressful," he replies. "But nothing I can't handle. How are things at Sutton Developments?"

"Same," I reply. "Charles is piling more on my shoulders every day. If I didn't know better, I'd think he finds it funny."

Alessandro gives a half-hearted smile. "Well, I imagine he wants to make sure you'll be ready to run things when he's retired. That's nothing to laugh at," he replies.

"Are we really going to sit here and talk about work?" I ask bluntly, unable to handle it anymore.

Alessandro uncrosses his legs and leans his arms on the table. "What would you prefer we discuss?"

"How was your trip?" I ask, not wanting to accuse him of anything directly.

He smiles faintly. "It was wonderful, until it wasn't. I had to cut it short and come back to work." He leans back in his chair. "How was your honeymoon?"

I give him a skeptical look and huff a dry laugh. "I'm entirely sure you don't want to hear about it," I reply. "I need to know something, but I don't know how to ask you, Alessandro."

He scrubs a hand over his face. "Then just ask."

I take a deep breath. "Did you bring Bryce's sister with you to Italy?"

He stares at me impassively. "Yes."

I'm not sure if I didn't expect the honesty, or if, deep down, I didn't really think I was right, but his answer is like a punch to the gut.

"How could you do that?" I bark at him.

The waiter chooses that moment to come back and take our orders. It gives me a moment to calm down, at least. Once he's gone, I give Alessandro a minute to respond, trying not to look like I want to smack him.

"Have you talked to her?" he finally asks.

"Not yet," I reply. "She's avoiding us. But I've known you longer, anyway, and I think I deserve an explanation."

"If it makes you feel better, she's avoiding me too," he says drily. "Though in my defense, I didn't think it would upset you."

"That you had a fling with my sister-in-law? That whatever happened upset her so badly she won't talk to anyone?" I have to work to keep from screeching the words at him.

The sadness in his eyes spreads, and his face falls. "I'm sorry," he replies. "I didn't intend for any of this to happen. But for what it's worth, it wasn't a fling. Not to me. Even if I didn't realize until it was too late that it was for her." And he looks so thoroughly miserable, I have no choice but to believe him.

"I may not be able to get ahold of her," I reply firmly, "but if this was just a fling to her, she wouldn't be this upset."

He raises his eyes to mine. "Do you really think so?"

The hope in his voice is evident, and I realize there's much more going on here than I imagined. "Alessandro," I gasp. "You're *in love* with her, aren't you?"

He shakes his head. "How can you be in love with someone who only thinks of you as their dirty secret?"

"You *are* in love with her." I'm in awe. I was sure after he'd given up on me that he'd gone back to dating casually, read man-whoring, wholly put off by relationships after everything we'd been through.

He sighs. "Yes."

"I'm seriously confused right now," I admit. "Let's back this up. What happened at our party?"

"I can't say it was love at first sight, if that's what you're asking. Even I'm not that clichéd. But as soon as I laid eyes on her, I *did* feel like I'd met her before. The feeling that I just *knew* her grew stronger with every minute we spent together." He sighs again, something I'm getting the sense he's done a lot of lately. "I think she was emotionally overwhelmed by your announcement and just needed to do something drastic. So when I invited her to come with me, I don't think it was because of me that she said yes."

"But you got close that week."

"I fell in love with her that week," he admits, shifting uncomfortably in his seat. "It's very strange, telling you these things. Knowing it upsets you. I didn't—"

I throw up a hand to stop him. "I was upset because I thought you were just working your charm on her, or using her for a good time or something," I explain. "I didn't know how you felt." I pause, thinking about what he's said. "Why do you think she thinks of you as her dirty secret?"

Alessandro smiles wryly. "Emily seems to believe she's got nothing to bring to the table in a relationship. Or, at least, that's what I thought was holding her back until she informed me she could never have a relationship with me because of her brother. That she only meant for us to be a 'vacation fling.' I'm afraid I said some things at that point that I'm not proud of."

Our food is delivered then, giving me time to process while we eat in silence. But I'm too distracted to care much about the food, and it's not long before I put down my fork.

"What could you have possibly said that would make her shut everyone out?" I muse out loud.

"It's not just what I said. It's also what she thinks I did."

My eyes meet his and he sets down his own fork.

"I was technically sharing a room with someone," he explains, "not that I spent much time in it. After our fight, I think she went looking for me there. As I understand it, a woman in our group I'd admitted to being previously involved with had been — what's the phrase? Ah, yes — shacking up with the other person sharing the room. Anyway, this woman and he were in the room, and she thought it was me in there with her. She left before I could correct the misunderstanding."

When he finishes, I'm gaping at him in disbelief. "So she thinks you had a fight, then went and fucked some other woman?"

He rolls his eyes to the ceiling and breathes deeply. "It sounds so much worse when you say it out loud."

"Well, it explains why she is so upset," I offer. "But it also convinces me you definitely weren't just a fling to her, Alessandro."

He looks back at me, again with that glint of hope. "You think?"

I laugh drily. "Yes, but I don't know that that helps you much. Because she wasn't wrong. Bryce is going to blow his lid. You'll be lucky if you survive long enough to convince her you aren't a disgusting prick."

Alessandro goes back to picking at his food. But I'm thoroughly done with mine. My brain has moved on to other things.

"We needn't ever upset him with the knowledge," he finally mutters. "What good would it do? She's even more stubborn than I am. She'll never listen. And even if she does, she made it abundantly clear that she doesn't feel the same about me."

I fold my arms on the table and lean forward. "Oh, we're going to tell him," I insist. "Because if we don't get him on board, Emily will never know what really happened. Until she does, you'll never know for sure what was possible. Is that what you really want?"

This time he tosses his fork down forcefully. "It doesn't matter what I want, dammit. Your husband is never going to let me anywhere near his sister after he learns of all this."

"He will," I assure him. "And then you're going to tell Emily what really happened. If she doesn't want to be with you after that, then at least you'll know it wasn't meant to be."

He stares at me for a minute, clearly confused and upset. "Why would you go to all this trouble?"

I grin gleefully. "Because once, when I'd given up hope, she was the obnoxious little thorn in my side. She meddled and meddled until Bryce and I got together. And now I'm going to return the favor. But I think the better question is, if you really love her, why wouldn't you?"

Alessandro smiles dimly. "Because she doesn't love me, Serafina. You may know her in many ways, but I've known her in a way you can't. She's still finding her way, and I think she's too scared of opening herself up to someone. I've been there. It's why..." he trails off, looking at me thoughtfully. "It's why all of us casually date, never letting things get serious enough to matter, never letting anyone affect us."

"Her walls aren't going to break themselves down," I reply firmly. "If she hadn't helped Bryce break mine down..." I shake my head, refusing to finish that thought. "If you'll let me, I'd like to do this. Please, Alessandro."

"I think it's cute that you're asking my permission. I know you quite well, Serafina, and I'm fairly certain you're going to do this whether I want you to or not," he replies with a wry smile.

That gets a laugh out of me. "Excellent," I reply, picking my fork back up. "Now let's eat. We're going to need the energy for what comes next."

He raises an eyebrow. "I sense I'm not going to like this."

I smile at him beatifically. "Not at first," I agree. "But you'll be glad once it's over." He looks at me, waiting for me to tell him what I've got planned. I shake my head and laugh. "I thought it would be obvious. We're going to tell Bryce everything."

Chapter 6 — Serafina

I've been nervous all afternoon since leaving Alessandro. Since promising to call him as soon as I'd prepared Bryce. But now, sitting on our living room couch, waiting for him to walk through the door, I still have no clue how to break this to him.

When the door clicks open just before six, I don't run to greet him like I normally would. I rise, unsteadily making my way to the entryway.

"Hey, baby," he calls, grinning at me across the open space. "How was your day?" He removes his suit jacket, revealing the gun holstered under his left arm.

"Fine," I reply vaguely. As I near, I point at the weapon. "Why do you still carry that thing? You're the boss now. Surely you don't pull security detail anymore?"

He raises an eyebrow at me. "It's never bothered you before," he remarks, undoing the holster and setting the whole thing down on the table next to do the door.

Yeah, it's never bothered me before. But I'd rather not tell him something that's going to piss him off while he's packing heat.

I go up on my toes to greet him with a kiss. "I was just asking," I reply nonchalantly, pressing my mouth to his. I slip my arms around him and sink into him, hoping to put him in as good a mood as possible.

"Mmm," he murmurs. "I missed you today." His hands slip over my backside, pulling me into him tightly. "Want to join me in the shower?"

I press my hands against his chest. "Maybe later," I reply. "But first I need to talk to you about something."

He draws his head back, giving me a suspicious look. It's the first time in recent memory I've passed up the chance to get him naked. "Everything okay?"

I roll my lips through my teeth. "It's about Emily."

"Okay, what about her?"

I step out of his embrace, tugging him by the hand into the living room. Once we're settled on the couch with one of my legs crooked in his lap, holding his hand in mine, I look up at him and take a deep breath. "I think I know why she won't talk to us. But I need you to promise not to freak out if I tell you."

Bryce laughs and undoes the top two buttons of his shirt, then leans back into the couch while stroking my leg. "This is about the Italian."

My mouth drops open. And I realize I was an idiot to think he wouldn't already know everything. He always knows everything. After all, that's kind of what he does for a living. The sight of me gaping like a fish makes him laugh harder.

"Seriously, babe," he says, then hooks his thumbs back, pointing at himself. "Security consultant."

I shake my head. "But why didn't you tell me you knew? *When* did you know?"

He shrugs, giving me a small smile. "You have zero poker face, Sera. When I made that joke about killing someone this weekend, it was written all over your face. It took me about two minutes to figure out where she was on her little trip and who she must've been there with."

Fuck. I forget sometimes exactly how damn observant he is.

"So why aren't you more upset about this?" I press. "You hate the guy."

Bryce shrugs. "I don't *hate* him," he starts, but is stopped short as I fold my arms over my chest and give him the most skeptical look I've got. "Okay, fine, I'm not his biggest fan. But I've long since learned to stay out of Em's business. And I know it was probably just some impulsive thing she did anyway. She doesn't do relationships. No sense freaking out over something that's not going anywhere."

"What do you mean, she doesn't 'do' relationships?" I demand. Suddenly, I'm angry on Alessandro's behalf.

Bryce pulls a reticent face. "She has her reasons."

"Ones that make it okay to toy with people's emotions?" I demand.

His eyebrows jump. "The Italian has emotions? There's a newsflash."

"Bryce," I say, a warning in my voice.

He puts his hands up. "Okay, okay, I didn't realize he actually cared about her." He pauses. "*Does* he actually care about her?"

I take a deep breath. "Yes," I reply softly. "I've never seen him like this. I think he really loves her."

"Wow. Didn't see that coming." He looks pensive about it.

"Does that change the way you feel about them?"

"I don't know," he admits. "I'd already written it off. But regardless of how he feels, he's got a mountain to climb to even get her to listen."

"You're the first hill," I point out.

"Me?" he asks in surprise.

"Yes, you, you big scary dork," I snap. "She told him she couldn't really date him because she didn't want to upset you."

"Pfff," Bryce scoffs. "Please. Em does what she wants. That's a total bullshit play."

"She may be your sister, baby, but I know a woman trying not to fall for Alessandro when I see one. I was that woman once," I remind him.

He grimaces. "Ugh, really?"

"Really," I confirm, not sure which part I'm validating. But the answer is the same for both anyway. "Why don't you tell me what's really holding her back?"

He sighs. "You and her are a lot alike," he grumbles. "Can't mind your own business, can you?" But by the small smile tugging at his lips I can tell he's not totally opposed to my meddling.

"Don't worry, I'll warn him that if he ever hurts her, you'll end him and all that crap," I promise.

He laughs. "Oh, don't worry about that," he assures me. "If he can get behind the walls of Fort Emily, I'll take care of that myself." He cricks his head to the side, cracking his neck. I roll my eyes at him.

"Whatever. Pissing contest later. Talk now."

But he still looks reticent. "She's going to be mad I told you."

I crawl into his lap, holding his face between my hands. "Don't worry about her right now. It's just you and me here," I say softly, grinding my hips into his. His mouth opens a fraction.

"You fight dirty," he breathes, running his hands down my back.

With a smile, I lean in, so my lips are hovering over his, my breasts grazing his chest. "I learned from the best."

With a smile, he plants a brief, chaste kiss on my lips, then pushes me back on his lap. "Short version? Emily's first boyfriend was bad news. And it didn't get a lot better from there."

"Which kind of bad news?" I ask delicately.

"The metalhead, drug-using, getting-locked-up-for-assault type," he replies grimly. "He hit her once. Only once, and that's what convinced her to leave. He was arrested for nearly beating a guy to death a month later."

I can't imagine a world where the feisty woman I know lets a guy hit her. Or where her protective older brother doesn't do something about it.

"What did you do to the guy?" I whisper.

Bryce shakes his head. "She was in college at the time, and I was deployed. By the time I came back, he was dead. Prison fight." The sorrow in his eyes is only a shadow of what I imagine Emily went through. "She's always been tough. But when I got home, she was even tougher than when I left. Doesn't take a lick of shit from anyone. Not sure how, but she's been in love twice since. Mostly just ended because the guys were too big of douches to be very good boyfriends. But ever since that first wreck, when she gets hurt or scared, she just withdraws for a while. Then she comes back like nothing ever happened. It just established some really bad patterns for her."

"I had no idea."

He runs his hands lightly down my arms. "She doesn't exactly open up to people, babe. It's not your fault you didn't know. Hell, it's not the Italian's fault either. If he really does have feelings for her, if he said something to her about it, that would be enough to send her running. She was just scared."

"Scared," I agree. "And hurt too." I relay everything Alessandro told me about their fight and her thinking he was with another woman after that.

Bryce lets out a low whistle.

"Yep, that'll do it."

"So what do I do?" I ask.

He considers me for a moment. "There's nothing you can do," he says simply.

"But I—"

He holds up a hand. "The Italian's got to. He needs to do what I should have done, instead of sending Emily in to do it for me."

I huff a small laugh. "Oh? And what's that?"

He sits up, drawing close, and looking deeply into my eyes. "He needs to do whatever it takes. Stand at her door shouting his feelings for the world to hear. Send her love letters through the cracks of her door all Harry Potter–style and shit. Let her see how fucking lost he is without her. That's what the dumbfucks before him never did. Fight for her."

His thumb skims my cheek, and I realize he's brushing away tears.

"I thought about doing all those things and more," he whispers. "I gave you too much space. He shouldn't make the same mistake."

I laugh through my tears. "Don't beat yourself up," I reply. "It turned out pretty good for us, in the end."

He smiles. "Yeah, but only because my sister couldn't stay out of it. But if you try to do that to her, she'll close up more. I know her. It has to be him. And he has to be unflinchingly patient and steadfast. Trust me."

I close my hand over his. "I do. Though I'm still not sure why you'd want to help Alessandro win her back."

He frowns. "If that's what makes my sister happy, who am I to stand in the way?"

I run my finger along his pouting lips, then replace it with my mouth. This man. When I pull away, he looks considerably less upset.

"You are the most amazing man I've ever known. I love you, Bryce Hoyt."

He graces me with his sunshine smile. "Love you too, baby. Now, if we're done talking about my sister, I need to be buried in you. Now."

He flips me onto my back next to him, grinding against me as I giggle in protest.

"No! Don't! Stop!" I screech amid the laughter.

His hand slips under my panties, stroking me. The sudden assault has me bowing into him in pleasure.

"Ohhh, don't stop," I moan with another giggle.

His mouth moves to my breast, teasing my nipple through my shirt. And I can't remember for the life of me what we were talking about.

Later that evening, though, when I'm no longer distracted, I call Alessandro. I can tell he's in shock that Bryce would so readily approve. I don't bother explaining that it's not exactly approval. But that if he really wants to get through to Emily, Bryce isn't standing in the way. And I relay exactly what Bryce told me he'd need to do. While I'm tempted to share why she's holding back, it's not my place. But I warn him that she's been hurt before, that it might take time, but not to give up if she's what he really wants. Unsure of whether he actually plans on pursuing her, I realize it's time for me to step back. The rest is up to Alessandro.

Chapter 7 — Emily

I stare at the plate of food for a full fifteen minutes before dumping it in the garbage. Can't say I haven't been trying. I take another sip of vodka from the bottle on the counter. It's worse this time. So much worse. I barely hear it when they knock anymore. Mom. Aunt Char. Bryce. Chad.

I settle onto the couch, absently picking up the guitar sitting there, strumming mindlessly. I can't bring myself to play anything else lately. Endlessly replaying that night.

Sometimes it makes me angry. Sometimes it makes me sad. But right now, I'm just numb. Thank you, vodka.

I think about leaving. But with no car, that leaves me with airplanes, boats, or trains. And I hate trains. Slow, cramped, and smelly. And airplanes are out of the question. Too many memories now. Maybe boats. But that would take effort I don't have to give right now. Damned in any case.

A sharp pain wakes me, and I look down. My index finger is bleeding from the endless strumming. I almost laugh. Good. Bleed, little finger. Let it all out.

I know I need to talk to someone, anyone. But to be honest with them, I'd have to be honest with myself. And that's just not worth it. None of it is worth it. Especially not him. Bastard.

I keep strumming. I keep bleeding. But I don't really care.

At some point there's a knock again. Not having kept track, I have no idea which of my regular tormenters it is, not that it matters.

Knock. Knockity-knock. Knockity-knock-knock-knock. I strum quietly in time with the beat.

"Emily, I can hear you."

It's Him. I stop strumming. I stop myself from yelling at him to go away. He will. And he doesn't need to know how drunk I am.

"Please, *Cara Mia*. I should've come after you sooner. You must know I didn't do what you think I did. It wasn't me in there with her, I swear it."

I laugh out loud, then clap a hand over my mouth. It's silent for a moment.

"I know you don't believe me. It sounds so trite. But it's true." His sigh is audible through the door. Oh, he's good. Excellent performance.

"There's so much I want to tell you," he continues. I tip my head back and forth. Doesn't matter. Still can't. Won't. Whatever. "I almost wrote you a letter. But I knew you'd tear it up the instant I slipped it under your door."

I smile. He's not wrong.

"I wanted to leave you alone. To let you yell at me when you were ready." There's a soft thud on the door. His head? His hand? I'm almost curious. "But your brother, he told me not to let you do this. To make you listen. It almost made me laugh, *Cara Mia*. He of all people should know that nobody can make you do anything."

Make me. The words ring through my head. *Back off*, I say. *Make me*, he says. I shake my head, putting my hands over my ears. *No. You're not allowed in my head anymore.*

Through my fingers I can tell Alessandro is still talking. It's not until the talking stops that his words sink in. My brother told him. But that can't possibly be true. Bryce wouldn't tell Alessandro anything of the sort. Would he? More lies. Or are they?

Just like I knew it would, his voice goes away. But now I have something else to keep me awake tonight.

* * *

I wake up cotton-mouthed, with a pounding headache. Geez. I'm never going to learn my limits with booze, am I? I get in the shower, hoping the hot water will do something for my aching head. But as soon as I'm in there, it wakes me up enough to remember that I had a visitor last night. And I remember enough of what he said to change my usual plans for the day of haplessly drinking and playing music.

Once I'm dried and dressed, I call Bryce.

"Oh, good, you're not dead," he greets me. "I take it the Italian must have paid you a visit then?"

I roll my eyes. Never one to mince words, my big brother. "Did you really send him here?"

"That I did. Now stop using me as an excuse. If you want to dump the bastard, step out of my shadow first. And while I'll deal if you decide not to, you know I'd be more than happy if you did."

"I don't know. You've got a pretty big shadow," I grumble. Seems like he's always up in my business anyway.

He laughs. "You're a big girl. Figure it out. But now that you've emerged, I expect you to be at brunch this Sunday. Mom's going out of her mind worrying about you. If you're not there and presentable I'm coming after you. For real this time."

"Fuck you," I grouse. No mercy, this one.

"Love you too, Em. See you Sunday." And he hangs up.

Guess my reign of solitude is at an end.

I find something presentable to wear and get ready to go out. I'm going to need food before I can deal with anything.

But when I open the door, I'm stopped short by an obscenely large vase full of purple hyacinths on my doorstep. I drag them inside, debating whether to throw them out. With a sigh, I pluck the card out. Might as well.

I never asked what your favorite flower is. I hope that you'll tell me someday. Forgive me, please, Cara Mia.

I make to tear up the card, but my gut protests. The rest of his words from last night come rushing back in a booze-stained swirl. And while I can't bring myself to get rid of his apology, I also can't bring myself to believe him. There's no point. It's over. Even if he's no longer my dirty secret, the fact remains that I never meant for it to turn into anything. Bryce is right. I'm going to have to dump him in a way that puts an end to things once and for all.

* * *

A solid lunch and a few texts with Sera later, and I'm headed to Alessandro's place. While it's less than a ten-minute bus ride, I'm too impatient to wait, so I walk the twenty-five or so minutes into downtown from Capitol Hill. For October the weather's not bad. Fifty-eight degrees and partly cloudy, it's the perfect day for jeans, a light flannel, and some cute sneakers. Not that I'm trying to look cute for him. Though I'm not above rubbing it in either.

He lives in one of the monstrous skyscrapers near the library, and the elevator ride up to his floor is annoyingly long.

Finally, I arrive and head down the long hall to his door. I have to talk myself through every step, still not sure exactly what I'm going to say. And where I find the courage to knock, I'll never know.

The door swings open moments after I do, and Alessandro stands there looking ridiculously perfect in a black T-shirt and black sweats. Why, why does he have to be so good-looking?

I clear my throat and deliver the words every man fears the most. "We need to talk."

One of his eyebrows jumps, but he moves quickly to hide his shock, stepping back to let me in.

"I'm glad you're here," he replies evenly. "Come in."

I step inside and check out his bachelor pad while he closes the door behind me. It's pretty freaking nice, with richly dark leather furniture, and huge windows that let in as much light as is possible for fall in Seattle.

"Can I get you something to drink?" he asks politely from beside me.

I turn toward him and shake my head. "No, thank you."

With a small nod, he moves into the living room, taking a seat on the largest couch. I pointedly sit in the slightly smaller one across from him.

"You're looking well," he remarks. "I was worried."

I roll my eyes. "Thanks, but I'm fine." God, I'm such a liar.

He runs a finger under his chin. "Really?" he asks, clearly not buying it.

I press my lips together. "On second thought, do you have any vodka?"

He stares at me unemotionally before rising. A minute later, he returns with two tumblers, each containing an inch of cold, clear liquid. He hands me one, and I shoot it back and set the glass down on the coffee table between us.

Alessandro settles on his couch, cradling the glass in his hand, and takes a deep breath. "Is this the part where you tell me that you don't care what really happened? That it's over?"

I look at him, shocked. "How did you know that's what I was going to say?"

He takes a sip of his shot, grimacing against the sting of the alcohol. "Because it's what I would say in your shoes."

I narrow my eyes at him, unsure of whether this is him accepting the situation or not. "So you know where I'm coming from then."

He tosses back the rest of his drink and sets the glass down. "So you know I didn't fuck Valentina, then?" he parries, looking me dead in the eye.

I squirm uncomfortably. "Yes." As much of an ass as he was that night, I think even then I knew that wasn't something he would do. That I was looking for a reason to run.

He looks at me like he knows. "And you know your brother isn't going to stand in the way of whatever it is you want?"

I purposely still myself, though it kills me. I have got to keep cool. "I was a little surprised that he seemed so willing to let the fox into the henhouse, but yes, I know that too. But that's exactly it. I don't want you, Alessandro."

He laughs. "Is that so?"

I shrug. "Yes?"

Both of his thick, dark eyebrows jump at that. "Then why did that sound like a question?"

"Look, it was just a vacation thing. Anything we were feeling was just being out of our reality. That's not a relationship."

"Well, that's bullshit, but let's humor you for a moment. That doesn't mean you don't want me. That just means you think you only wanted me because of where we were."

His forthrightness makes me laugh. "Okay," I concede. "But that also assumes I want a relationship at all. Which I don't."

"Also bullshit," he insists.

I'm starting to get annoyed. "You think you know what I want better than I do?"

He sighs and rises, coming around the table to settle on the couch next to me.

"Yes. Because once again, you're simply fighting against what you really want, *Cara Mia*."

This close, I can see his long, dark lashes over his deep brown eyes. I can see his desire there. And his restraint.

"You're wrong this time," I assert. "I'm not looking for complicated. And you, sir, complicate things."

His eyes drop to my mouth, and I tighten inside. Ugh. He's right. I do still want him. But it's just physical. We're just too much alike, and I'm already exhausted by a short conversation with him.

"Then I'll make it simple," he replies, leaning in so I get a full whiff of his spicy scent. "Let me take you on a date. Here, in our reality. If you still feel like it's not what you want, then I'll have to accept that."

"You'll have to accept that now," I reply stubbornly.

He laughs. "You're afraid."

"Pfff. Am not." Even I realize I sound like a petulant child, so I work on softening my expression. "Exactly what do you think I'm afraid of? You? Hardly."

His full mouth pulls to the side in a smile. "That I'm right. That now that I'm not your dirty secret anymore, it's your own stubbornness holding you back from seeing how good we are together."

I don't even think about considering his words. He's just trouble. "Ugh, fine, whatever. If one date is what it will take to prove I'm right, then that's what we'll do." I stand up. "Coming?"

He stands up, looking down at his clothes. "I'm not exactly dressed for the occasion. And it's a weekday. I have to get back to work. Are you busy Saturday night?"

I frown, sticking my chin out. He's going to make me admit my only plans were with a bottle of booze.

I sigh heavily. "I guess I could make that work."

He smiles so widely it crinkles the corners of his eyes. "Then it's a date."

"Fine." I rise, heading to the door. I make to open it, but he puts a hand up to stop me. He's uncomfortably close.

His eyes search mine. "Do you have a black tie–appropriate dress?"

"Yes," I reply, hugging my arms around myself protectively.

His eyes settle on my lips, and I resist the urge to lick them. "Good. I'll pick you up at seven then."

I raise an eyebrow, but he says nothing more, simply opening the door. It takes everything I've got to tear my eyes from his and walk out the door.

Just before I cross the threshold, I turn to him. "Peonies." He looks at me questioningly. "They're my favorite flower." I don't wait for a response. I leave. Before he can see me blush.

Chapter 8 — Emily

Two days. Two days of going back and forth between almost cancelling and asking myself if he's right. I want to sink back into a drunken stupor and avoid thinking too hard about it, but I've probably done enough of that lately.

So at seven on Saturday evening, here I sit, dressed in a deep blue lace and crystal gown, my chestnut waves tamed into a gentle cascade, nervous as I can ever remember being. Too nervous even to play anything to soothe myself.

When the knock on the door comes, I take a deep breath, rise, and smooth my dress. Opening the door is my first huge mistake. Because it gives me a full view of Alessandro, looking more devastatingly handsome than any man I've ever seen. And he's holding a huge bouquet of the most beautiful pink peonies I've ever seen.

He looks just as stunned, staring at me as I take him in, in his tailored black tux, with a black shirt, vest, and tie. He looks lean, and strong, and so hopeful I already feel guilty.

"You look…" he trails off, seemingly unable to form words.

I look down at the neckline that plunges to just above my belly button, the sheer sleeves and leg panels that show swaths of my pale skin under them. One of the perks of being skinny and flat-chested — I don't have to worry about falling out of the daring neckline. But maybe it was a bad choice.

"Too risqué?" I ask, blushing. "I can go change."

He closes his mouth and shakes his head, his eyes returning to mine. "No," he says hoarsely. "You're perfect." He extends the flowers. "These are for you. Though they're not half as beautiful as you are."

"Yeah, okay," I reply, rolling my eyes. I take the flowers anyway, quickly darting into the kitchen to put them in water. I purposely don't invite him in. But I'm back in a flash, only to find him uncomfortably standing on the doorstep. Good. He should be uncomfortable.

He gives me an uneasy smile, extending a hand. "Shall we?"

I slip my hand into his somewhat reluctantly and close the door behind me. "Where are we headed?" I try to sound casual, but I'm kind of dying to know what we're all dressed up for.

"I was thinking the café and wine bar a few blocks from here," he replies. "If you're not too hungry and don't mind walking?"

"That depends. Is it raining?"

He laughs. "For once, no. I wouldn't have asked if it were."

"Okay, then, that sounds perfect. Let's go."

We walk the few blocks in silence. I've been to the café a few times, but it's not a place I go often. It seems a bit laidback for our formal attire, but I can't argue that the wine is fantastic. We order a few appetizers as well, and the stare-off begins.

"So, this is awkward."

He chuckles. "There you go, saying what's on your mind again."

I shrug. "How's work? Everything okay with whatever made you cut your vacation short?"

"It will be fine," he replies with a note of annoyance in his voice. "Running your own business is not without its sacrifices. Though I had hoped for more of a break. Perhaps once things have died down a bit more. How is work for you?"

My eyes drop to my lap. "I quit."

"You quit?" His shocked tone is enough to make me look back up at him. "I thought you loved working there."

I chew on my upper lip and take a sip of wine. "Things change."

"In three weeks?" he asks.

I glare back at him defiantly. "Yes."

"Why did you quit, Emily?"

I jut my chin out. "It's not what I want to do for the rest of my life."

"Oh?" He raises an eyebrow. "And have you decided what you *do* want to do for the rest of your life, then?" A hint of a smile plays around his mouth.

I tug at my hair. "Not exactly."

"I see." He tilts his head and gives me an appraising look. "With your talent and your intelligence, *Cara Mia*, you could do whatever you want. I hope you know that."

This time I don't stop the eye roll. "You've barely heard me play."

He shrugs. "What can I say? I know talent when I see it."

"Are you always so blindly positive?" I grouse.

"I can be a negative asshole, if you'd prefer."

And I can't help it, it makes me laugh.

He smiles, clearly pleased to see me lightening up. I decide to at least try not to be such a sourpuss. But he just brings emotions out in me I can't control sometimes.

"Do you like classical music?" he asks as our appetizers are delivered.

"Of course," I reply.

"Good," he replies, digging in with a smile.

"Why?" I ask, suddenly suspicious.

"Because we're going to the symphony tonight."

My eyes go wide. "Seriously?"

He laughs. "Seriously. Is that okay?"

I blink hard, willing myself not to tear up. I've dated enough musicians to start a freaking orchestra, but not a single one has ever taken me to the symphony. Dingy little hole-in-the-wall clubs, sure. But never anything as overwhelmingly moving, or pricey, as the symphony. I've only been a handful of times with my parents.

I watch him as he continues eating, suddenly unsure that I can resist him if he's going to pull out all the stops like this.

The feeling only intensifies after we've finished and are headed into Benaroya Hall, just a couple blocks from the restaurant. The crowds of well-dressed patrons stream into the building, and I can't help feeling a bit like a princess. Alessandro leads me patiently by the hand, giving me plenty of time to ascend the steps in a way that doesn't snag the delicate material of my gown.

As I climb the last step, he squeezes my hand and shakes his head.

"What?" I ask.

"You'll just tell me to stop the charming shtick," he says with a smile.

I narrow my eyes at him. "You're probably right."

With a chuckle, he leads me inside and to our seats. My jaw drops when I see how close we'll be.

"How'd you get these seats? They're amazing," I breathe softly into his ear as he takes his seat next to me.

He turns a dazzling smile on me. "I told you. Music is one of my great loves. I've been a donor and subscriber for years. I'm not completely full of shit, you know."

I put my hand over my mouth, unwilling to burst into laughter in such a setting. As the lights dim, he turns from me to focus on the stage. I stare at him, remembering my thoughts the first night I met him. Wondering if he really was more than the man I thought him to be. But maybe it's because he is, and so much more, that I'm so unsure.

Before my emotions can completely carry me off, the music starts to swell, and it does the job for me. Mozart's Jupiter Symphony begins, and I'm carried into a world that only music can transport me to. My heart swells with the beauty of it, tears of joy leaking unbidden from my eyes. The few times I look over at Alessandro, he's, for once, not focused on me at all, seemingly similarly transported by the music.

And when it's over, I'm riding high on the excitement of the experience. "That was unbelievable," I sigh as I follow him out into the cool night. A little too cool. I shudder at the abrupt change of temperature. Seeing my discomfort, Alessandro removes his jacket and drapes it around my shoulders.

The lingering warmth and the scent of him settles over me. I look up at him, trying not to connect all the emotion that the music evoked to him. But he brings out his own response in me. And in this moment, that's pretty hard to deny.

I step up onto my toes and press my mouth to his. The familiar warmth makes me tighten inside. But he only returns the kiss for a moment before pressing back.

"Come, I'll walk you home," he says in a restrained tone.

I try not to be annoyed. Really, I do. But it's just the same as when we arrived in Italy. He's holding back, thinking too much. I can tell.

By the time we make it to my front door, I'm so over it all. I shrug out of his jacket, handing it back.

"I had fun. Thanks."

"You're welcome."

"Okay, well, take care then." I turn around, fishing my keys out of my bag.

But he has other ideas. He grabs me gently by the arms, turning me to face him.

"Tell me why."

"Why what?" I ask impatiently.

"Why do I scare you so?"

I feel the anger rise in me. But just as quickly, I realize he's right. He scares the shit out of me with his intensity. His insistence that we're perfect for each other. His expectations.

"You want things from me I can't give you."

"Bullshit." His dark eyes are filled with fire. "You're scared to give what you have."

"Yes," I admit with a tired laugh. To him. To myself. "I've been down this road before. It's never turned out well for me. Can't we just enjoy each other? Without giving ... more?"

"But you've given it to others." His mouth turns down, and the sorrow there is like a punch to the gut.

Again, he's not wrong. I've loved men before who could never give me back what I wanted to give them. But maybe the tables have turned.

Tears prick at the back of my eyes. "I'm sorry, I can't give you what you want," I repeat.

"You mean, you can't give me what you think I deserve."

"Is there a difference?"

He strokes a finger under his chin. "Yes. But perhaps you're not ready to see that yet."

"It doesn't matter. I don't belong with someone like you," I reply a little more angrily than I intended. I close my eyes, pushing back the tears, the rage. The truth is something I didn't expect. He cares about me in a way I struggle to even care for myself. He's way too good for me. He makes me wish I was more. Better. And I can't handle that kind of pressure. That's what's making me angry. I'm mad at myself for not being what he needs. I shove it all down deep, steel myself, and look up into his eyes.

He's strangely calm, watching my internal battle play out on my face. When I catch his eye, he gives me a hard look.

"Tell me honestly that you don't want me," he says in a low, even tone.

"It's not that simple," I hedge.

He steps closer, lifting my chin to force me to look in his eyes. "It never is, *Cara Mia*. But that doesn't mean it's not worth fighting for." He kisses me gently, completely in control this time as he ends it quickly. It leaves me wanting, brief as it was.

I shake my head, not knowing what to say. He's still watching me intently, with those dark, expressive eyes of his. He lifts his hand to my cheek, stroking it gently.

"I had an amazing night with you. Go, get some sleep. Think about things. I'll call you tomorrow."

I raise an eyebrow at him. "What, you're not even going to try to come in?"

He shakes his head and laughs. He looks down at me, with a dangerously sexy glint in his eye. "We're not going to fuck so you don't have to think, *Cara Mia*."

My eyes go wide. How did he know that that was exactly what I wanted?

"I see you," he says. "Just as you see me. Remember that."

With that, he turns and walks away. I go inside, dumbstruck as I undress and clean up for bed. And when I go to sleep, try though I might, all I see is his face.

* * *

Sunday morning brings no rest. Literally. I have to drag ass out of bed and get ready for brunch at Mom's. And prepare myself for the inquisition. Not going would only be worse, because then Bryce would be pissed, *and* I'd still have to make an appearance.

I resign myself to the trip, and I'm about to call for a ride when Sera texts asking if I want to go with them. I accept, though I'm not as excited by the prospect as I normally would be. Though it does occur to me if I could get her on her own, she'd be the best person to talk to about this whole mess. After all, she knows me pretty well by now. And obviously she knows Alessandro in ways pretty much nobody else I could talk to would.

Ugh. I realize that means I *do* want to talk about it. He's getting under my skin, the persistent bastard.

When I get downstairs to meet Sera and Bryce, I'm actually pretty relieved to see them both. They're out of the car, and Sera gets to me first, wrapping me in a big hug.

"Hey," she greets me.

"Hey."

Bryce gives me a little wave. I let Sera go and throw myself bodily into him, hugging him tightly.

"Oof," he grunts. "Geez, Em."

I let him go and swing a fake punch toward his soft spot. He instinctively reaches out to stop me with a surprised look on his face. I stop my fist in midair, laughing. "Hey, bro."

He shakes his head and climbs in the back seat, and Sera gets in on the driver's side. "Hop in," she invites, gesturing to the front passenger door.

"Huh," I remark, climbing into the passenger seat. "I feel special."

Sera pulls out, giving Bryce a look in the rearview mirror. "Just pretend he's not here. You know, if you need to talk before we get to your mom's."

"Ugh," I remark. "She's pretty worried, huh?"

"We all are," she says quietly. "But you look good, Em. I missed you."

I shoot her a smile. "Missed you guys too. Did you have fun in Italy at least?" Sera turns bright red and Bryce chuckles. "Ew, never mind." We all burst out laughing.

"So, you and Alessandro, huh?" Sera asks pointedly.

I heave a sigh. "Sort of? I don't know."

"Well, for what it's worth, he's pretty into you," she remarks drily.

I snort. "Yeah, I got that much, funny enough." I look down into my hands.

"You can say what you want. Bryce has promised to keep his mouth shut. Right, babe?" Bryce says nothing and Sera smiles mischievously. "See?"

I shoot him a smile and he wrinkles his nose at me and sticks out his tongue. I can't help but laugh.

"It's fine. I've never exactly held back around him anyway," I tease.

"You have no idea," Bryce grumbles in Sera's direction. She shoots him a warning look and he pointedly shuts his mouth.

"Come on, Em. I'm here. Talk to me. I know Alessandro has his issues, but he's a good guy. And if you're really not interested in him, that's one thing. But if you think you're upsetting Bryce or I—"

"No," I cut her off. "I don't think that at all." I let out a frustrated sigh. "I know he's a good guy. And I know he's into me. And I'm into him. I just don't think I'm good for him."

Sera looks over at me, astonished, then quickly returns her eyes to the road. Bryce, to his credit, makes not a peep.

"That's the last thing I expected to be holding you back," she says bluntly. "I mean, I don't want to dismiss your feelings or anything, but you're pretty freaking amazing, Em. I mean, seriously. He'd be lucky to be with you."

I roll my eyes. "Thanks," I reply, unable to keep the sarcasm out of my voice.

"You think I'd lie to you?"

"No, I think you have love blinders on," I retort. "And I appreciate that. But honestly. I'm a freaking mess. What do I have to offer anyone right now? I've got no job, no prospects, and every long-term relationship I've had has blown up in my face. He's gorgeous, smart, successful, and has women tripping over themselves to be with him. What do I have to offer someone like that?"

Even voicing the doubts has me squirming. I've never lacked confidence like this. But something about my whole life right now is making me feel like I'm doomed to fail. At everything.

"He's not in love with those women; he's in love with you," Sera insists.

My eyebrows jump and I spin toward her, my jaw practically on the floor. "He's *what*?"

Bryce face-palms. "Way to scare her, babe."

I don't even look at Bryce. I'm glaring down Sera. And she looks pretty damn nervous. "Are you assuming or did he tell you that?"

She clears her throat. "I'm guessing he didn't tell you that, then."

"Um, that would be a big nope," I reply angrily. "I can't believe you guys even talked about all of this behind my back. Oh my god, I'm so humiliated." I put my hands over my face. This is just too much.

I'm silent the rest of the way to Mom's, and neither of them says another word.

When we get there, Bryce gets out first, then Sera. I lean forward and put my head on the dashboard, trying not to cry.

A minute later, Bryce climbs in the driver's seat, moving it back all the way to accommodate his long legs. I look up in surprise when he starts the car.

"What are you doing?" I ask, wiping at the tears that have mercilessly found their way out.

Bryce shakes his head and looks at me. "I'm taking you back," he explains quietly. "Unless you want to go in there?" His expression is apologetic and full of concern.

"I don't," I agree. "Please, just get me out of here."

We make the drive in silence. I stare out the window as we cross the bridge, wishing I was on one of the ships in the bay, headed far away from here. But when the car stops, it's not at my place. It takes me a minute to realize where we are. Before I can even react, Bryce speaks.

"I know you're scared, Em. And your life isn't what you expected." He turns to me and lays a hand over mine. "But I know you. You're falling for this guy. I've never seen that scare you, though, so I think that means this might be the kind of love that's exactly what you need. That will give you the strength and support to become the person you want to be." He pauses, letting his words sink in as the tears flow down my face. He gives my hand a squeeze. "And if it doesn't, and he breaks your heart, I'll break his fucking kneecaps. Deal?"

Through the tears, I laugh. My stupid big brother. Well, he's not so stupid. He knows me better than anyone. Or, almost anyone. Because I'm pretty sure Alessandro tried to tell me all of that, too. I was just too scared to listen.

"Deal."

Bryce grins. "Come on."

He gets out of the car and I follow, letting him lead me inside. "How do you even know where he lives?" I ask as I wipe the tears from my face.

Bryce shoots me a smirk. "Seriously?"

I roll my eyes. "Never mind." We get in the elevator. As we near Alessandro's floor, I look over at him. "Hey, Bryce?"

He looks at me furtively. "Yeah?"

"Thanks."

He shoots an arm out, wrapping it around my neck and bringing me in for a hug. "I've got you, Em."

We arrive, and Bryce gets out first. When he gets to Alessandro's door, he pulls me behind him so he's blocking me from view and hammers on it hard.

I hear the door open a moment later, and I realize I'd give anything to see the look on Alessandro's face. But I don't move, trusting whatever my big bro has planned.

"Ah. The giant. How nice. To what do I owe the pleasure?" If I didn't know him better, I'd say he sounded sincere, but I don't miss the undertone of his distaste.

"I'm only going to say this once. Hurt my sister and it'll be the last thing you ever do." His voice is low and menacing. I've heard him use the tone before. Never a good thing. I crack a smile behind his broad back.

I hear Alessandro heave a deep sigh. "Trust me, if she'd let me, I'd spend my life doing everything I could to keep her from ever hurting again."

"Huh. Well, cute words. Good luck with that." Bryce steps aside and gives me a look. "I'll make your excuses to Mom."

I nod and give him a small wave. He waves back as he heads to the elevator.

I turn, and Alessandro is leaning against his doorway, arms crossed over his black T-shirt.

"Hi," I say meekly.

His face is unreadable. "*Ciao.*"

"Did you mean that?" I ask. "What you said to my brother?"

"I don't think this is the best place to have this conversation," he hedges, stepping back. "Why don't you come in?"

I follow him in quietly. He sits by himself in the leather chair at the end of the two couches. My stomach sinks as I take a seat on the smaller couch. He's clearly distancing himself from me. So maybe he didn't mean what he said. Maybe he was just placating Bryce.

Alessandro scrubs his hands over his face. "Can you please tell me what is going on? Why your brother felt the need to threaten me?"

I take a deep breath, deciding to take the advice of my wise, if not annoyingly perfect, big brother.

"I've been scared shitless," I admit. "I've been adrift, for years really. As if my perfect brother getting married and taking over the family business wasn't bad enough, meeting you just made me feel completely inadequate." He starts to protest, but I hold up a hand. "You're amazing, Alessandro. I didn't get how someone like you could care about me. I feel like I've got nothing to offer. I'm such a mess. I don't know what I want to do. I'm like a balloon floating in the wind. But Bryce convinced me I could do with an anchor. Someone who makes me stronger. I don't know, I'm losing the metaphor. Am I making any sense?"

He leans back. "Yes." He pushes out a breath. "I feel like a failure."

"What? No," I object. "*I'm* the failure. I'm such a mess I can't even let someone care about me. And I'm so sorry."

Alessandro looks at me with a sad smile. "No, *Cara Mia*. I've failed you if I let you think for one moment that I wouldn't be the lucky one here. You are like nobody I've ever met. You're beautiful, honest, funny, talented, and so smart. You keep me on my toes."

"With my crazy," I grumble, starting to smile, nonetheless.

He laughs. "Yes, exactly," he agrees. "My crazy, beautiful woman." He frowns. "So your brother convinced you to come here but then threatened me. Am I missing something?"

"You still don't get him at all, do you?" I ask, laughing. "That's his way of saying he approves."

He looks at me skeptically. "Are you sure?"

I rise, moving to settle on his lap. He reaches for me, pulling me into his embrace. "I'm sure," I reply. "And I'm sorry. I'm my own worst enemy. I do this. I tell myself I don't deserve things that make me happy and then I do everything I can to drive them away."

He holds my face in his hand, stroking my cheek. "We're going to have to work on that," he murmurs.

"We're going to have to work on a lot of things," I agree. "But you were right before. It may not be simple, but this is something worth fighting for."

"Hmmm. So I guess I'm not your dirty secret anymore," he says, fighting a smile.

"You can be my dirty something else instead," I murmur, covering his lips with mine, pulling at his clothes. Because I may have given him what he wants, but now I'm going to get what I want.

He doesn't resist, letting me pull his shirt off as he runs his hands over my breasts, my hips, my ass. I rise, stripping completely in seconds, then sink down and run my hands over his chest.

He slips his hand between my legs, stroking my core as he sucks on the tips of my breasts. He lifts me gently, then eases me onto the coffee table, kicking off his sweats. I twitch with anticipation as he bends over me, kissing his way from my mouth downward.

"*Leccamela tutta*," I plead. He laughs, but obliges, immediately disappearing between my legs and licking me into a frenzy. Before I can finish, he rises to kiss me, hovering just out of reach.

"Do you want to feel me?" he asks softly.

I bite down on my lip, glancing down at his full, hard, beautiful cock. "Yes," I agree. "Just you."

He wastes no time, burying himself in me. I throw my head back.

"You feel unbelievable, *Cara Mia*," he moans.

I nod in response, hitching my heels behind his backside, urging him on. He holds himself over me carefully as he rides me. And all I can do is hang on as he takes us both over the edge.

When we're done, and cleaned up, he stretches out on the sofa, still completely naked, gesturing for me to join him. Gladly, I stretch my body out next to his.

"Sera accidentally told me something," I confess.

He ceases stroking my arm and raises an eyebrow. "Do I want to know?"

I laugh. "It was about us," I reassure him. "She said you're in love with me."

"Ah."

"And you told Bryce you'd spend your life keeping me from being hurt."

He smiles and resumes stroking my arm. "I did."

I tilt my head back so I can look him full in the face.

"Does it scare you?" he asks softly.

I take a steadying breath. "Yes. But only because I'm falling for you too," I admit. "So maybe give me a little time to get used to it."

He presses his lips together and his eyes glitter fiercely. "*Amore mio*," he breathes. "Take all the time you need. I'm not going anywhere."

And I know enough Italian to translate that one. He loves me. I can't say it doesn't scare me. But at least now it's in a good way.

"I still don't understand why," I admit. "I think you might be a little crazy too."

He smiles so widely I can't help smiling back. "Yes, we're both a little crazy. It's what makes us so good together," he replies. "But as to why … why does anyone love someone? Some things are just meant to be." He thinks about it for a moment. "I realized it when you left me. But I think I might have loved you the moment you agreed to run away with me." He nuzzles his nose into my neck, lightly kissing its length. I stroke my fingers through his hair.

"Thank you for not giving up on me," I breathe into his ear.

"It's a good thing I'm more stubborn than you are," he teases, kissing me.

"Mmmm," I moan as he continues to stroke and kiss me. "You're going to need to be. I've got a lot of things to figure out. I'm going to need someone who is stubborn and patient enough to get through to me when I need a good talking to."

He laughs. "Yes, well, those are important qualities," he allows. "But I think there may be a better way to get your attention."

"Oh? How's that?" Though I think I know the answer, but damn do I want him to show me.

He presses his leg between mine, silently asking for entry. I open for him, and he slides between my legs, flipping me on my back under him. His semi-hard cock pushes between my thighs, and a moan bursts out of me.

"Something like this," he murmurs as he enters me.

As he fills me, it's like a switch flips inside me, and tears of joy fill my eyes as he makes love to me. He sees me. He gets me. He loves me. Really knowing it and accepting it, I feel free. Free to love him. Crazy, passionately, completely. He's the happiness I never thought I deserved.

Epilogue – Alessandro

Ten years later…

"Dammit, Emily," I groan.

"Don't stop," she begs. "We've got time."

I lean around her to glance at the microwave clock. "We're already late," I reply.

She pouts, sliding her dress up. "You started it." She licks her lips, and I'm screwed.

With a growl, I pull her ass toward me and lay her down on the counter. I run my hand down her chest before sinking my fingers into her pussy while I undo my zipper with my other hand. I quickly replace my hand with my cock and bury it in her. I have to steady myself. The first thrust is always tight and sweet. Even after all this time, it nearly undoes me.

She writhes, grabbing at her breasts with one hand, working herself above where I'm thrusting with the other. So uninhibited, so sexy. I help her tease her nipples as I take her. I don't hold back, tilting into her exactly the way I know will have her screaming her orgasm in no time. Mere moments later, I'm not disappointed, and I follow her over as I explode inside her.

"See? That didn't take long," she teases, climbing down and heading to clean up.

"Sure, but now you're going to your niece's sixth birthday party with just-fucked hair," I joke. I follow her into the bathroom to see her smoothing her gorgeous chestnut waves back into place.

"Like it never happened," she murmurs, shooting me a fake dirty look in the mirror.

I grab her ass, slipping my hand under her skirt into the wetness still between her legs.

"The evidence suggests otherwise," I whisper in her ear.

"Mhm," she agrees, adjusting her makeup. "But you know you love it when I walk around with your cum dripping out of me."

I was just about to leave, but her words have me grabbing her from behind, running my hands all over her. "You're going to be the death of me," I say against the soft skin of her neck.

She smiles, finishes getting ready, and pulls me out of the house.

As we drive over the West Seattle Bridge, she rolls her window down and lets her arm drag through the warm summer air.

"You look happy," I tell her with a smile.

"What's not to be happy about? It's a beautiful day," she replies. "And we haven't seen Bryce, Sera, and the kids in weeks."

"And I imagine those three weeks in Paris didn't hurt, either," I reply drily.

She shoots me a huge smile. "Nope, definitely not."

I laugh, gunning the engine, and whipping around a bend. She giggles gleefully as I accelerate through a curve. "I love this car," she cries into the wind.

And like I have every day since she agreed to be mine, I think to myself, *Damn, I love this woman.*

We finally arrive, only half an hour late thanks to my crazy driving.

The kids rush out to greet their favorite aunt, and I hang back, taking the presents out of the back seat. Their father's distaste for me seems to have been passed down, as the children have never shown much interest in me. Still, I'm happy to let them crowd around Emily, knowing how much she enjoys these moments.

Serafina waddles out of the gate to the back yard, her hugely pregnant belly preceding her.

I go to her and wrap my arms around her carefully. "You look beautiful."

She smiles up at me. "Thanks. I feel like a whale."

Emily joins us, the children circling her. "Hey, Sera. How are you feeling?"

"She wants to get the darn thing out of her already," Hattie, their nine-year-old, proclaims. We all laugh.

Katherine, the birthday girl, pulls at Emily's hand. "Auntie Em, come see my princess party."

"Oooh, princesses are my favorite," Emily coos at her. "Which one are you, Kitty?"

The little girl, who looks so endearingly like her mother, rolls her eyes and points at her dress. "Duh, I'm the purple one."

We all share looks of barely suppressed laughter and let the children lead us into the backyard. True to her word, it's a princess paradise, with crowned little girls in dresses everywhere, piles of princess-wrapped presents, and a bouncy castle.

Emily leans down and scoops up the youngest, three-year-old Landon, named for Bryce and Emily's father. She carries him along as Kitty pulls her toward the food, wanting to show off her cake. I add Kitty's present to the pile, a little purple ukulele that Emily had made just for her.

I spot Bryce, the only man in a sea of tiny girls and a few mothers who have tagged along. Predictably, he's manning the barbecue. And he's dressed like a fucking prince. I roll my eyes, getting it out of my system before he notices me.

"Well, that's a little clichéd," I joke as I approach, gesturing at his outfit as I hand him the "present" I brought for him.

He gives me a tolerant smile, cracking open one of the ice-cold beers I just gave him. "Thanks." He passes me one. I open it and we drink in silence.

It gets to me after a bit. "Where's your brother-in-law?" I ask abruptly, noting Sera's brother's absence.

"He and his partner are traveling," he replies, flipping a burger. "They're taking an art tour of Europe."

"Ah. Well, that sounds like more fun than a kid's birthday party."

Bryce smirks at me. "How was your trip to Paris?" he asks.

"It was great. Just what we needed. Emily was reticent to leave the music shop to her assistant, but it all went fine."

Bryce shrugs. "I know, she wouldn't shut up about it. But I get it. She's worked hard to build that place. It's her baby."

I shoot him a look at his choice of words. I'd thought we were long over the "When are you guys getting married and having kids?" part of our lives. But I say nothing, and the big bastard just smirks back at me, letting the small needling stand. Thankfully, he says nothing further on the subject.

"When is baby number four supposed to make its appearance?" I ask, watching Sera struggle to take Landon from Emily so Emily can help Kitty open her present. Bryce and Emily's mother appears suddenly, wrestling the little guy away as the ukulele appears and they all fawn over the gift.

"A few weeks," he murmurs, watching his wife. "But damn if she doesn't look good pregnant."

I roll my eyes, knowing he's paying no attention to me.

"I saw that."

I laugh and shake my head. "I'm going to go help the women."

"With what?"

I shrug, smile, and walk away.

I approach Emily, now sitting next to Kitty on the ground as she teaches her how to play the tiny instrument. She looks radiant, her flowery sundress hugging her body, the sun shining on her face as she laughs at the little girl's clear enjoyment of her gift.

She looks up at me and smiles. It takes my damn breath away.

"I know that look," she says with a warning in her voice.

I wink at her. "You just look so good," I tease. "So happy."

She rises to her feet and tucks herself against me, wrapping her arms around my back and looking up into my face. "I am."

I look down at Kitty. "Not getting any ideas, are you?"

She laughs. "You ask me that every time. No." She puts her mouth to my ear. "I like being able to fuck you as often and loudly as I like with no tiny interruptions." She kisses my earlobe and it sends shivers down my spine. She pulls back a little. "I'm starting to think you might want me to get ideas."

I huff a laugh. "You know I love you, no matter what life brings us," I hedge. I lean in, also to whisper in her ear. "But you're not going to get me to fuck you at a children's birthday party, no matter how sexy you are or what dirty things you whisper in my ear."

She pulls away, laughing gleefully. "We'll see about that."

"We'll see about what?" Sera asks, appearing from the back door to the house with a lighter in one hand and a stack of paper plates in the other. I quickly move to take them from her, for which she shoots me a grateful look. "Thanks. Even small chores are tough right now. I can't wait for this to be over. For good, this time."

"Oh? This is the last then?" I ask, a teasing note in my voice.

She settles herself onto the padded swing next to the house. "Damn straight. This was a surprise baby, anyway. And I'm forty. Four seems like a good number of kids, anyway, doesn't it?" she muses.

I shrug. "I'm surprised you have time for it all. You both run your own companies, after all."

Sera snorts. "Don't kid yourself. There's no such thing as 'time for it all.' We run ourselves ragged every damned day and we're lucky if we even cover the basics."

I frown, laying a hand over hers. "Serafina, I'm so sorry. We should help more—"

"No," she interrupts, squeezing my hand. "I wasn't complaining. We have plenty of help. Rebecca lives here, for crying out loud." She gestures at Bryce and Emily's mother, who is now studiously tidying discarded wrapping material. "I even tolerate my mother's occasional whim to drop by, because every little bit helps, and the kids love her." She presses her lips together. I know how hot and cold their relationship has been over the years, so I say nothing. "We are ridiculously blessed, and I love my life." She looks up at her husband who is staring at us across the yard. She waves and smiles at him as Landon finds us and starts to crawl in what little lap she has left. She lifts him up, cradling him to her chest. "Really, I wouldn't have it any other way."

"I'm glad you're happy," I tell her sincerely. "It's all I ever wanted for you."

She tilts her head. "What about you and Emily?"

I look up at Emily, who is leading the children loudly in a song now, her beautiful voice carrying on the wind. "We are happier than I ever thought possible. I'm a very lucky man."

"Good," Sera concedes, letting her son down and struggling to her feet. "See that you keep it that way. Because Bryce is still ready to tear you limb from limb if you hurt her." She pats me consolingly on the back. "Time for cake."

I watch her walk away, meeting Bryce to ready the cake. When all the kids crowd around them, Bryce lifts Kitty to blow out her candles and everyone cheers. Kitty gives her father a big kiss before he sets her down to descend upon the giant, icing-slathered confection. I watch Emily too, helping Sera cut the cake. They all look so happy.

But as the throng of tiny princesses brim over with the excitement of dessert being served, madness returns, and Emily extracts herself with a roll of her eyes to join me on the sidelines. I fold her into my embrace, and we wait until things have died down to rejoin the crowd.

Sera, Bryce, and the girls happily greet us as we do, and we allow ourselves to sink into this little slice of familial bliss.

Enjoyable though it was, when we get back home, I breathe a sigh of relief.

"It's so quiet," I remark happily.

"What, was a dozen little girls screaming all afternoon wearing on you?" Emily teases, heading into our bathroom to undress.

"A little," I admit, kicking off my shoes and following her. I lay on the big, soft bed, quietly watching her. When she removes her sundress, I realize she wasn't wearing any underwear. "*Cara Mia*, you're a naughty girl."

"What? The dress covered enough so nobody could tell. Besides, I was hoping you'd figure it out much, much sooner," she says with an affected pout, coming to the edge of the bed. She crawls next to me, snuggling against me. "But I had a good time anyway. Everyone seemed to be doing so well."

I stroke her hair, drifting a little after the heat and exertion of the day. "Mmmm, yes they did. They have a different kind of crazy going on there," I murmur sleepily.

"Do you still like our crazy?" she asks, a note of concern in her voice.

My eyes snap open, and I turn her head so I can look into her eyes. "Love. I love our crazy." I press my lips to hers, easing my tongue into her beautiful mouth. She responds, rubbing against me. Alas, it doesn't stir me in the way I'd like it to. "I think I'm getting too old to take you three times a day."

"And I never thought I'd still want you three times a day after so long. But I'm happy just being here with you," she assures me with a gentle kiss.

"You're amazing," I murmur. But I can't let it rest. I roll on top of her, rubbing into her center. "Say it."

She looks at me, confused for a moment before realizing what I want her to say. What I want her to ask.

"*Leccamela tutta*," she whispers.

With a devilish smile, I waste no time pleasuring her. Claiming her with my mouth and hands, body and soul. Because she touches mine more every day. And there's nothing I won't do to make her happy for as long as she'll let me. And as I taste her, as she gives herself to me so completely and with abandon, I know if I have my way, it'll be forever.

Acknowledgements

Like this novella, I'll make this short and sweet. First thanks always go to my patient husband for making my writing more of a priority than I do sometimes. Much love to Lindsey Powell for alpha reading this bad boy! A huge thank you to Ms. Katie Douglas for showing me how a slightly different take on the cover looked so much better, and for being a mega awesome beta reader (again)! Mad props to my homegirl Andrea Hopkins for beta reading and writing some steamy goodness of her own. Eternal love and gratitude to Jenny Gardner for her awesome editing skills. And last, but not least, endless thanks to the readers who loved Bryce so much I had to find a way to give you just a little more.

Want more? Check out Melanie A. Smith's latest romantic suspense standalone novel

Everybody Lies

Read on for a sneak peek!

Prologue — Frankie

Dolly sits on the floor next to Pandy. They drink tea while I wait for Momma and Jack. Jack is Momma's new friend. Momma says he is a nice man, but I don't like him. He smells like cigarettes. And he brings me peppermint candies. I hate peppermint candies. Momma says it's because he likes me. But I know she's lying.

"Francesca, dinner is ready, come to the table, *now*," Momma calls from the kitchen.

I watch Momma and Jack carry plates to the table, so I get up. I wait for Jack to go back in the kitchen, then I sit down in my chair. The plastic is squishy and sticky under my bottom.

Momma and Jack bring the rest of the food and it's finally time to eat. Tea parties always make me hungry. Momma gives me a big spoon of the beef and noodles. *Stro-guh-noff.* I say it slowly and quietly to myself. Jack gives me a funny look. He's always giving me funny looks that Momma doesn't notice. Just like the kids at school.

"How was school today?" Momma asks me.

"My teacher says I'm the best reader she's ever seen in first grade," I answer proudly, happy that she finally asked. "She gave me a book called *Little Women*."

Momma looks like she doesn't believe me. "I think you probably misunderstood her. That book is far too advanced for you. You're only six."

I frown, unhappy that she thinks I'm not a good enough reader for *Little Women*. "But I've already read some of it, and I like it," I protest.

"Don't lie," Jack snaps at me. He's been mean before, but I don't like being called a liar, and I can't stop myself from saying something back this time.

"I'm *not* lying," I insist. I jump down from the chair to get the book from my backpack, so I can prove it.

"Francesca Marie, I did not give you permission to leave the table," Momma yells. I stop, knowing I'll be in big trouble if I don't.

"But Momma, I can show you —"

"I said, *sit down*," she insists. "I'm going to have a talk with your teacher tomorrow about age-appropriate books. You'll bring it to me after dinner. I won't have you reading it anymore."

"Oh please, Sam, she's *not* reading that book. She's obviously lying," Jack says again.

"I'm not a liar, you're a liar." The words come out of my mouth before I can stop them.

Momma's eyes go wide. Jack's face turns red, but she puts her hand up and I know she wants to talk instead.

"You apologize right now, young lady. You know better than to speak to an adult that way." Momma's voice is too quiet.

I know that quiet. But I'm still mad because I'm not lying. And I know Jack lied to her. And even though she told me never to use my gift to hurt people, I don't care right now.

"But he lied to you last week when you asked why he was gone so long. He wasn't taking out the garbage. *He* is the liar," I scream back.

Jack isn't red anymore. Now he's white. And that makes me happy because I know that means he's scared. Momma is quiet now. Jack looks at her.

"She's just a kid. She doesn't know what she's talking about." *Lie.* "You gonna let her talk to me like that?" Jack's voice sounds scared too. Because I told on him.

"Francesca, go to your room, please," Momma says softly but firmly.

I swallow hard and nod. I'm quiet as a mouse as I unstick myself from the chair and stand up.

"She doesn't know what she's talking about," Jack says again. *Lie.*

I back slowly into the living room.

"I *was* takin' out the garbage, just like you told me to. I just got sidetracked talkin' to Jimmy." *Lies.*

The little voice inside me always knows. Now that they can't see me anymore, I turn around and run to my bedroom. I close myself in my room and hide in my closet, hoping Momma isn't mad at me.

I listen to their muffled voices. They get louder. They yell for a long time. Then the front door slams and the pictures on the wall shake.

Finally, Momma comes. The closet door slides open and she sits on the floor next to me. She looks really mad.

"I'm sorry, Momma," I whisper. "I didn't mean to, it just came out."

"I know, and I'm glad you told me," she says, sounding very tired. "But you have to keep it to yourself. The things you know can cause trouble."

I don't understand. "You really didn't want to know that Jack lied to you?"

"That's not the point. If people know what you can do, you won't be safe anymore," she says.

"Why not?" I ask.

My mother brushes a long strand of my dark hair behind my ear. "Because they'll think you're a freak, Francesca," she says impatiently. "And we don't need that kind of attention. Besides, most people really don't want to know the truth anyway."

"But I always want to know the truth. How do you know what you should and shouldn't do if you don't know the truth?"

"You can never know the whole truth, Francesca. People lie on purpose, but they also lie by accident. And people lie to themselves. There is no such thing as just the truth," she explains. "I think you're old enough now to learn the only real truth. That everybody lies."

Chapter 1 — Frankie

The room is dimly lit. I stand against the wall, my feet shoulder-width apart, both hands on the gun that hangs loosely in front of me. My eyes scan the other side of the room through my lightly tinted glasses, watching the shadowy figures come and go. Waiting.

Finally, I catch sight of my target. I exhale as I confidently lift the weapon, aim, and fire. And I nail the motherfucker right between the eyes.

The lights snap back to full brightness abruptly. I holster my gun and pull my ear protection off.

"Dammit, Frankie, you're supposed to get him in the chest," Mac grumbles, coming out from behind the safety glass.

I shoot him a grin. "That's hardly a challenge," I scoff.

Mac scratches at his flaming red beard and scowls at me. "Don't be thick," he chides. "You're not a goddamn sniper — you're supposed to be learning defensive shooting. If this was in your little club it wouldn't be so easy. It'd be dark, loud, an' a whole hell of a lot harder to hit your target. Aim for the torso. Harder to miss and shoot some drunk fecker instead."

I can tell he's really annoyed, because his Irish brogue is thicker than usual. And I can't argue that he has a point. "Fine, fine," I reply. "Reset?"

We've been at it nearly two hours, but I can't help enjoying something I'm so damn good at.

Mac shakes his head. "Another day. I'm starved," he insists, rubbing his round belly.

"I guess I could eat," I allow. With a sigh I remove my safety glasses and pull out my hair band, letting my bright pink waves cascade back over my shoulders. I work my fingers through the roots at the back of my head, rubbing the tension from the spot as we pack it out of the range.

"Tacos?" Mac asks, climbing into his junky old pickup truck that's probably as old as he is. And that's saying something. You'd think for being such a successful guy he'd have a nicer set of wheels. But it's part of his charm, I suppose.

"You know me, I'll never say no to tacos," I agree as the old engine rumbles to life. "So who is the meeting with this afternoon?"

Mac stares straight ahead, navigating traffic on the backstreets. "New money. He wants in on the casino buyout."

"Ah. So you're not looking for my skills in wooing moneybags out of his cash. You want me to tell you if he's dirty."

Mac is one of the few people who knows about my ability. And only because I know he can keep his mouth shut.

"Got it in one," Mac agrees with a smirk. "You still sure you don't want in on the deal?"

I laugh. Mac is a persistent old bastard.

"I've got my hands full at Baltia, but thanks," I reply drily. I'm not sure why he even asked. He knows I live and breathe that club these days.

"Awww, come on, for old time's sake?" he presses.

I can't decide if he's teasing or not. "All my cash is tied up right now," I insist. "And that'd be one hell of a favor for old time's sake. Even for the return."

Mac mentored me toward my goal of owning a nightclub. Having more than thirty years' experience in almost every type of adult entertainment business that exists, from casinos to bars and nightclubs to strip clubs, he took me on as his assistant and trained me. A little too well, perhaps. I got out from under his wing as soon as I felt confident that I knew what I needed to in order to go for it. And while he taught me a lot, he expected more. I was his work horse for the better part of a decade. Not that I'm complaining, but I've already got enough on my plate.

"How is the club? You gonna be in the red at the end of year one?" he asks curiously.

I laugh. "Of course I am," I reply. "But I'll be making money hand over fist by the end of year two. Don't you worry."

"There you go getting cocky again," he warns with a shake of his head.

I press my lips together to suppress a smile. He's not wrong — I'm probably being overly confident. But then, I was a good student and I've done my homework. And the club is finally taking off, as per plan. The plan that's been ten years in the making. I think I've earned a little confidence.

* * *

The meeting is quick, and Mac's investor was clean. Just a young, enthusiastic tech millionaire looking to diversify. Don't get me wrong, he dropped plenty of lies in the meeting, just nothing unusual. The same bullshit everyone spouts.

I go home to shower, change, and eat before heading to the club. It's a Saturday night, always our biggest night of the week, so I opt for something "club dressy" but still comfortable enough. If I've learned anything these last eight months, it's that running a nightclub is practically a sport, but one you have to look good while doing.

I opt for black pants with enough cling to be sexy, but plenty of give in case I need to kick some ass. Metaphorical ass, of course. We have bouncers who handle the other stuff.

My shiny purple, halter-neck corset-top is also both alluring and still holds everything in properly without being sweltering. I roll my long, pink locks up into a simple twist and pin it in place. The halter and hair-up combo has the bonus of showing off the half-sleeve tattoos on both of my arms that connect over my upper-back. A pair of black, four-inch platform boots adds to the dangerously hot look but also puts me at an even six feet tall. Perfect for seeing eye-to-eye with most males who might think they can intimidate me.

And I'm not just talking about patrons. Being a female nightclub owner who looks considerably younger than my thirty-four years with tattoos, piercings, and crazy colored hair, well, just about everybody challenges me at one point or another. My employees. My suppliers. The deejays, band managers, agents, dancers, and other entertainers. Everybody. It's why my two biggest hobbies are boxing and shooting. You can't be too careful or too prepared, I say.

As soon as I'm inside, everything else falls away as it always does, and I've got my game face on. It's three hours until doors open at ten p.m., but most of the crew is already bustling around, getting everything ready for the night. Bartenders are checking stock, the cleaning team is working on the floors and bathrooms, and Ace, my stage manager, is talking to who I presume to be the band manager for tonight's act.

I watch everyone from next to the coat check for a minute, admiring the scene. This club was dying when I bought it, and I've worked my ass off to bring it back to life. It took forever to clean up all the old concert posters on the wall with fill-ins and a coat of lacquer, making it look less like a fading rock club and more like a purposely styled, modern tribute to the club's history. The old wood paneling was replaced with a sleek, gothic print wallpaper with dark, heavy curtains at the entrances to match. The old bar to the left of the entrance was completely ripped out, allowing us to fill the whole wall with a streamlined, steel designed bar-front onto which we could project any number of shapes, colors, and images throughout the night. The bar-height tables and chairs spanning the deck across the front of the club were all replaced with a similar design to the look of the bar itself.

But the sunken dance floor behind the seating area was simply refinished, its dark wood polished of scuffs, and it gleams with a new sheen. The stage at the back of the venue was also mostly just spruced up. I didn't want to kill what had made this club famous in the first place. The acts that have played here over the years are legendary.

Every nick and dent on the stage are commemorations of their collective performances. Thankfully we've managed to keep the interest of some of the hottest bands around, blessedly smoothing the transition of ownership.

I spot my club manager, Nils, heading toward me from the hall on the other side of the bar that leads to the back offices. The tall, lanky Swede swaggers across the floor like he owns it. A former runway model, I think he just can't help it. But his good looks and charm are the shiny outside. Inside, he's a shrewd and precise club-managing machine. I wouldn't have survived this long without him.

"Mr. Larsson," I greet him in mock formality.

He does approving elevator eyes over me as he approaches. I return the favor. His fitted, designer black slacks and black button-front shirt are perfectly tailored. His shirt is unbuttoned just enough to show off his hairless, sculpted chest but doesn't give away *too* much. And his patterned dress shoes probably cost more than my entire outfit. He is, undoubtedly, ridiculously hot. Though far too much of a pretty boy to be my type. Which is yet another reason he was the best pick for the job.

"Ms. Greco," he retorts in a saucy tone, leaning in to kiss me on the cheek, and as usual I note that he smells better than most women I know. His shoulder-length blond hair tickles my collarbone as he pulls away.

I tip my head toward Ace, who is standing on stage with his hands in his pockets, looking at his shoes while the guy he's talking to gesticulates wildly. I can't tell from here if Ace is upset or not.

"What's going on there?" I ask curiously.

Nils gives the pair a glance and shakes his head. "That's Nick Pappas. He manages a bunch of acts we'll be hosting. I understand he used to do business with the previous owners as well. He's a real piece of work."

"Aren't they all?" I ask with a sigh. "Do I need to step in?"

Nils shrugs nonchalantly. "Couldn't hurt."

I give him a smirk, because his reserved, Swedish politeness always cracks me up. And I really know that's Nils-speak for, "Yes, please, go schmooze so I don't have to be the one to brown-nose this guy."

I check my makeup in the mirrored bar behind Nils's back and am pleased that I can see the smoky eye and bright red lip that are my go-to are still perfectly done. Heading down the stairs, I can feel Nils's eyes on my back. I assume he must have had it out with Mr. Pappas already, because he's clearly very interested in how I do with him.

Ace looks up as I approach, relief blossoming over his face. Since Mr. Pappas's back is to me, he doesn't notice as I hop the step up to the elevated platform. He is still gesturing wildly as he babbles.

"Gentlemen," I interrupt. "How are things going?"

Ace looks like he could kiss me, and I press my lips together, so I don't laugh. Mr. Pappas finally stops talking and spins around. Short and dark, his olive skin is greasy, and his suit is cheap.

"I think we have a misunderstanding about the —" Ace is cut off by Mr. Pappas whipping back around and glaring him into submission. But then, Ace is a go-with-the-flow guy, not really into confrontation. His grungy jeans, seventies band T-shirts, and hippie vibe certainly speak to that. He's great with the musicians. But stuck-up assholes like this guy don't really show him much respect, unfortunately.

"What junior over here isn't getting, is that I *specifically* requested separate restroom facilities for my guys. Now, you've done this before, and I don't understand what the goddamn problem is," Mr. Pappas spits. He looks me up and down. "Why don't you go get your boss? I'm sure he can straighten this out."

I take a subtle breath in through my nose and let all the things I can't say run through my head quickly before I respond. *He's about five minutes younger than you, asshole; no you didn't; and no, we haven't.* My next thought, however, I can say.

"You're looking at her," I respond with a sweet smile, extending my hand. "Francesca Greco."

Mr. Pappas's jaw drops momentarily as he stares hard at my chest, but he recovers quickly, roughly grabbing my hand. His shake is overly firm, and I suppress the urge to roll my eyes.

"Well, good," he grumbles. "Yeah. It's, uh, nice to meet you." He drops my hand and rolls his shoulders, eyes still fixated on my breasts. "So about the facilities."

My mouth twitches as I suppress an annoyed sneer. "I understand the previous owners may have been able to provide that; however, with bringing things up to code, unfortunately those restrooms are now shared between my employees and the performers, leaving the restrooms on the other side of the building dedicated to customers," I explain. "I apologize for the inconvenience, but I assure you my employees will not get in the way of your client's use of the facilities."

If I thought that was going to placate him, I was sorely mistaken. He turns as red as my lipstick, looking me in the eyes for the first time, and I know this is going to take every ounce of charm I possess.

"I was promised *dedicated facilities*," he all but yells in my face. *Lie.*

I fight the urge to roll my eyes at the inner voice. I didn't really need it to know he's full of shit.

"Do you remember who promised you that?" I ask, still sweet.

He blinks hard. "Well, no, but —"

"Okay, did you get it in writing then?" I press.

He scowls. "Well, no, but —"

"And you do understand that we're legally required to comply with health and safety codes that govern the purpose and use of facilities as allowed by our permitting and inspections," I continue.

"Well, yes, but —"

"And I know you wouldn't want us to risk getting shut down because we were caught violating those codes, since my club manager tells me you have other acts booked here in the future," I reply.

His shoulders slump, and if he had a tail, it would be between his legs. "Of course not," he grumbles.

"Good, then we're in agreement that your client will use the same facilities as per usual, and our employees will do their best to stay out of their way," I say with a smile. I lay a hand on his arm. "I appreciate it, Mr. Pappas. Not everyone understands the long list of rules we have to follow. You must be very good at what you do, knowing so much about clubs and all."

In my head it's said in a much more sarcastic tone. But out loud I manage to sound sincere, or a good impression of it anyway, and it has the desired effect. He perks up and puffs out his chest a little and Ace's eyes go wide with mirth.

"Yeah, I do," Mr. Pappas replies. "I'm glad I could help." His eyes drop back down south of my face, and I know he's calmed down and the storm has passed.

"Good," I reply brightly. "Well, it was a pleasure to meet you, Mr. Pappas. Please be sure to let me know if there's anything else I can do to help. But right now I should check in with my manager to make sure our VIP area is set up for the band."

"Uh, yeah, yeah, it was good meeting you too," Mr. Pappas replies, clearly a little confused as to what just happened. He looks between Ace and me for a few seconds before shaking his head and going backstage.

Ace bursts into giggles. "Thanks, boss," he says between snorts.

One of the roadies looks up from setting up the drum kit. "That guy's a dick," he says in a low voice. "I'm glad you didn't let him push you around."

I shrug. "I've seen worse," I assure him. I turn back to Ace. "And next time come get me or Nils sooner, okay? Between Nils's charm and these tits, we have all the weapons we need to distract asstwats like that."

The roadie snorts and Ace offers an apologetic smile. I shake my head and wander off to find Nils to talk promoters.

* * *

By midnight I can barely hear myself think. The band is in full swing and the whole club is packed wall to wall. It's actually my favorite part of the night. Being a human lie detector makes one-on-one conversations exhausting and irritating after a while. But being alone is a special kind of torture for me too. Being in a crowd, though, is strangely soothing. The energy, the excitement, the mass of bodies moving to the same beat, with the same purpose. It invigorates me. Always has. I let my hips sway as I lean against the railing, longing to lose myself in the crowd below me as they rage to the intensity of the music. Being boss has its downsides.

But it's been a good night overall so far for the club, so I really can't complain. Great take at the door and from ticket presales, and that's not even accounting for alcohol sales yet. Very few fake IDs, no fights, no drunk people passed out in corners. Well, maybe one or two. But Nils is pretty good at getting the bouncers on things like that before I even notice.

I'm perched in the corner of the VIP balcony, reveling in the atmosphere and scanning the crowd when I see Nils making his way past the velvet ropes and up the stairs. He's clearly headed for me. I give him a questioning look as he approaches.

When he gets to me he leans his mouth to my ear. "Johnny says there's a guy at the bar asking about you."

I look up into his ice blue eyes and raise an eyebrow as if to say, *So? A lot of guys ask about me.* There had been a few articles and news pieces when I bought the club and in the following months as we renovated. Great press, but they'd brought out some weirdos. Nils just shakes his head and motions for me to follow him. This one must be different.

At the bottom of the stairs, Nils pushes me toward the bar before returning to his rounds. Confused, I slip behind the bar and tap Johnny on the shoulder. He holds up a finger letting me know he's finishing the order he's working on.

I look down the length of the bar trying to spot whoever could be asking after me. In case it's someone I actually do know. But since the bar covers the whole wall of the club, it's hard to see everyone vying for a place at the counter, trying to get the attention of one of the four bartenders on duty. Not to mention it's dark, loud, and I'm starting to lose steam ahead of the second wind I usually get around this time.

Johnny finishes up and pulls me by the hand through the service door into the private storage area behind the bar we use for the security monitors. The doors are heavy enough to muffle the sound so we can hear each other. Johnny grabs a bottle of water and slumps into a high-backed chair at the bank of monitors on the far wall displaying feeds from the various security cameras around the club.

"Nils told you there's a guy looking for you?" he checks. He leans his broad shoulders into the soft backrest.

Johnny's short, dark hair is sweaty, his collared dark blue polo shirt also slightly damp. I resist the urge to chastise him for sweating all over the chair. We all sweat buckets every night. It comes with the territory. So instead, I nod and take the chair next to him.

His dark eyes flick up to the farthest monitor, showing the opposite end of the bar than we'd been on. He puts his finger under a large, hulking guy seated at a stool pulled into the corner. "That guy."

I squint at the image. He looks big. Dark hair. Dark shirt. Lots of tattoos. But his head is bowed, his face hidden from the camera.

"He asked for me? What did he say that made you have Nils come get me?"

Johnny is usually my first line of fending off the creepers, so I'm curious why he thinks this one is legit.

"He didn't ask for you. Mentioned you is more like it. But he called you Frankie, and he's been sitting there all night like he's waiting for something," Johnny replies, finishing his bottle of water. "I'm gonna hit the head before I go back out. Cover me and put eyes on him. Dave knows what's up, just let him know before you go over there." Johnny gets up and heads toward the door on the opposite wall leading to the staff restrooms that had been the subject of heated debate earlier this evening.

"I need exact words, Johnny," I call after him, staring at the screen and trying to discern more about the mystery man.

"He said, 'This is a cool club. It's Frankie Greco's place, right?' That's it." Johnny disappears to the bathrooms.

Now I understand why it raised a flag. There are precious few people who call me Frankie. Mac, my best friend Emma, and my family. That's it. Nobody at the club calls me Frankie. None of the news outlets had either, I'm sure of that. Not that it's a super uncommon nickname for Francesca. But it's just enough to be odd, without being threatening, exactly. Only one way to find out who this guy is and what he wants. With a shake of my head I get back up, throw an apron on, and tuck a few escaped pink strands back into place.

Heading back through the door, I poke Dave as I pass him to work the opposite end of the bar. He barely looks up, but I see him nod and send Jess back down toward Johnny's area to cover. I pass the fourth bartender, Peter, and he barely acknowledges my passing as he struggles to keep up with the throng.

I focus on paring down the line that's formed in Johnny's absence. After serving half a dozen drinks there's a small lull, so I lean against the back of the bar nonchalantly and grab a bottle of water. I scan the bar as if I'm just checking on everyone. The guy is so tucked into the corner, he's the last thing I see. But this time I'm only ten feet away from him, so I get a good look. Or I would have, had our gazes not locked as soon as mine settled on him. His eyes are dark and intense, and I get the sense he's been watching me the whole time.

Unexpectedly, my breath catches in my throat and it's like someone stuffed cotton in my ears. All the noise around me drops into the background. I struggle to breathe, telling myself it's an adrenaline response. He's not "mainstream" handsome, but he's attractive in a way that makes my insides tighten nonetheless. He has dark hair that is short on the sides, but long and wild on top. His jaw is a little too square and has a significant five-o-clock shadow, his nose is perfectly straight, but his full mouth is crooked under it. His thick eyebrows are set over his big, dark eyes in a way that makes him look like he's laughing. But the muscled and tattooed arms that extend out of his short-sleeved black T-shirt are no joke. And I wish I could say I'd seen him before, but there's not even a hint of recognition. Well, beyond my body recognizing that it would like to see more of that perfect physique hinted at under his tight-fitting shirt.

Before it can be classified as gawking, I stroll over to him, pretending to respond to his look as if he were asking for service. *Oh, I'd be glad to service him all right.* I can't help the thought, but I internally chastise myself for it anyway. I've never fucked a customer, and I don't plan to start with my dark, alluring, and potentially creepy stalker.

I lean in and use my carefully practiced bartender-in-a-loud-club voice. "Need anything?" I ask as casually as I can.

One of his eyebrows flicks up and he smirks, pointing at the empty beer bottle in his hand. The look is so ridiculously sexy that a flush creeps through me. I swallow hard and nod, taking the empty bottle from him. I reach behind me into the cooler and grab a new one, removing the cap as he watches before handing it to him.

He tosses a bill on the counter as he accepts the beer and takes a long pull. I pocket the cash and give him change. And before things pick up again, I decide to just go for it.

"I heard you're looking for Frankie Greco."

He sets his beer down and chuckles. "That's some grapevine you've got here."

His voice is deep and luscious and it sends shivers down my spine. God, why am I reacting to him this way? Down, girl. It's not like there aren't heaps of gorgeous men in here every night. Thankfully, I've had a lot of practice on my poker face, so I shrug in response, not wavering. He gives me an appraising look.

"You're her?" he asks skeptically, raising one of his thick brows.

I raise my eyebrow right back. "Maybe. You a friend of Mac's?"

He's the only one I can think of that might send this slab of a man into my club asking after Frankie Greco. But it's also bait.

"Yeah, Mac mentioned this was your place," he replies casually. *Lie.*

The familiar internal voice is like a punch in the gut, even though I was expecting it.

"Try again," I say tightly.

His eyes grow hard and he gives me a look somewhere between cautious and ravenous. But before he can respond I'm distracted by a wave of frat boys asking for shots. When I glance back at the corner, a lone twenty-dollar bill sits on the counter and the mystery man is gone.

Chapter 2 — Julian

Fuck. That round ass, come-fuck-me pink hair, and those gorgeous red lips that I can't stop thinking about having wrapped around my cock completely distracted me. And when those velvety blue eyes locked on me, I swear I almost came in my fucking pants. Control is practically my middle name, and I'm not some wet-behind-the-ears kid looking for a quick fuck in a dirty club bathroom. But fuck me if I couldn't breathe properly from that moment on.

Much less think and work the situation like I usually would. Because there was no guessing the most alluring woman I'd ever locked eyes on owned the fucking club. And it made me sloppy. I should've known not to show my hand. I'm normally much more subtle than that. I have to be. It's my job. She's just a job.

I'm totally fucked.

About the Author

Melanie A. Smith is author of *The Safeguarded Heart* Series. A voracious reader and lifelong writer, Melanie's writing began at a young age with short stories and poetry. Having completed a bachelor of science in electrical engineering at the University of California, Los Angeles, and a master's in business administration at the University of Washington, her writing abilities were mainly utilized for technical documents as a lead engineer for the Boeing Company, where she worked for ten years.

After shifting careers to domestic engineering and property management in 2015, she eventually found a balance where she was able to return to writing fiction.

Melanie is also a Mensan and enjoys spending time with her family, cooking, and driving with the windows down and the stereo cranked up loud.

Learn more about Melanie at melanieasmithauthor.com or follow her on social media at:

Instagram: instagram.com/melanieasmithauthor
Facebook: http://fb.me/MelanieASmithAuthor
Twitter: https://twitter.com/MelASmithAuthor
Goodreads:
https://www.goodreads.com/author/show/18088778.Melanie_A_S
mith
Tumblr: http://melanieasmithauthor.tumblr.com/

Books by Melanie A. Smith

The Safeguarded Heart Series
The Safeguarded Heart
All of Me
Never Forget
Her Dirty Secret
Recipes from the Heart: A Companion to the Safeguarded Heart Series

Standalone Romance Novels
Everybody Lies

A Note from the Author

If you enjoyed this book, I would greatly appreciate if you would take a few moments to leave a review, even if it's just a sentence or two saying that you like the book and why. Reviews are valuable feedback that let both the author and other readers know that the book is an enjoyable read. When you leave a positive review it also lets the vendor know that the book is worth promoting, as the more reviews a book receives, the more they will recommend it to other readers. Regardless, thank you for reading this book, and for your support!

Printed in Great
Britain
by Amazon